BORGES

AND THE ETERNAL ORANGUTANS

Also by Luis Fernando Verissimo
Available from New Directions

The Club of Angels

BORGES AND THE ETERNAL ORANGUTANS

Luis Fernando Verissimo

Translated from the Portuguese by
Margaret Jull Costa

A New Directions Book

Manufactured in the United States of America
New Directions Books are printed on acid-free paper.
First published as a New Directions Paperbook (NDP1012) in 2005.
Published simultaneously in Canada by Penguin Books Canada Limited.

First published as *Borges e os orangotangos eternos* by Companhia das Letras, São
Paulo, 2000.

Published by arrangement with Dr. Ray-Güde Mertin, Literarische Agentur,
Germany, and The Harvill Press, London.

This book was published with the assistance of *Ministério da Cultura do
Brasil/Fundação Biblioteca Nacional/Departamento Nacional do Livro.*

Library of Congress Cataloging-in-Publication Data

Verissimo, Luis Fernando, 1936-
  [Borges e os orangotangos eternos. English]
  Borges and the eternal orangutans / by Luis Fernando Verissimo ; translated
from the Portuguese by Margaret Jull Costa.
    p. cm.
  ISBN 0-8112-1592-X (alk. paper)
  1. Borges, Jorge Luis, 1899—-Fiction. I. Costa, Margaret Jull. II. Title.
PQ9698.32.E73B6713 2005
869.3'42—dc22   2004028203

New Directions Books are published for James Laughlin
by New Directions Publishing Corporation
80 Eighth Avenue, New York 10011

Irritated, Unwin stopped him.

"Don't multiply the mysteries," he said. "Mysteries should be simple. Remember Poe's stolen letter, remember Zangwill's locked room." "Or complex," replied Dunraven. "Remember the Universe."

Jorge Luis Borges, *"Abenjacán el Bojarí, dead in his labyrinth"*

Contents

The Crime

I WILL TRY TO BE YOUR EYES, JORGE. I AM FOLLOWING THE advice you gave me when we said goodbye: "Write, and you will remember." I will try to remember, with more exactitude this time, so that you can see what I saw, so that you can unveil the mystery and arrive at the truth. We always write in order to remember the truth. When we invent, it is only in order to remember the truth more exactly.

Geography is destiny. If Buenos Aires were not so close to Porto Alegre, none of this would have happened, but I did not see that I was being subtly summoned or that this story needed me in order to be written. I did not see that I was being plunged headfirst into the plot, like a pen into an inkwell.

The circumstances of my visit to Buenos Aires were, as I now know, planned with all the care of someone setting

3

a trap for a particular animal. At the time, however, enthusiasm blinded me to this. I did not realise that I had been chosen as an accessory to a crime, as neutral and innocent as the mirrors in a room.

The 1985 Israfel Society Conference, the first meeting of Edgar Allan Poe specialists to be held outside the northern hemisphere, was to take place in Buenos Aires, less than a thousand kilometres from my apartment in Bonfim, and was, therefore, within the budget of a poor translator and teacher of English (which, as you know, is what I am). One of the invited speakers was to be Joachim Rotkopf, who was to lecture on the origins of European surrealism to be found in Poe's work, precisely the topic that had provoked the controversy with Professor Xavier Urquiza from Mendoza, and that had kept me so amused in the pages of *The Gold-Bug*, the Society journal. All this seemed to me a mere accumulation of happy and irresistible coincidences. I decided not to resist. At least, I thought I decided.

I am fifty years old. I have led a cloistered life, "without adventures or surprises", as you put it in your poem. Like you, master. A sheltered life spent among books, and into which only rarely did the unexpected enter like a tiger. Not that I am an innocent. I am a sceptic, books have trained me in every category of disbelief and caution when confronted by illogicality. I could never have believed that destiny was calling me by name, that everything had been decided for me and before me by some hidden Borges, that my role was waiting for me, just as Mallarmé's *vide papier* was waiting for his poems.

The prospect of hearing the Argentinian's comments on the lecture by the German with whom I had corresponded, but whom I did not know personally, was enough in itself to justify the price of the air fare to Buenos Aires (paid for on credit). The conference would take place in July, when my students of English would be taking refuge in their hyperactive hormones, so as to protect themselves from the cold, thus enabling me to have a holiday. No urgent translation required my attention, at least nothing that could not wait a week, the duration of the conference.

The final coincidence: one day after the arrival of the journal containing both the remarkable announcement that the 1985 Israfel Society Conference had been transferred from Baltimore to Buenos Aires and instructions on how interested parties should apply, my cat Aleph died. Not from any discernible cause, but merely out of consideration for the old bachelor who had taken him in. Aleph was the only obstacle to my making the trip, because, now that my Aunt Raquel had gone into a home, there was no-one I could leave him with. Aleph's death convinced me not to miss this never-to-be-repeated opportunity. Yet even his all too convenient demise failed to arouse my suspicions.

Everything that happened to me there in Buenos Aires I owe, in some way, to Aleph's death. Or to geographical destiny. Or to the God behind the God who moves the God who moves the player who moves the pieces and begins the round of dust and time and sleep and dying in your poem, Jorge. Or to the designs of an ancient plot set in motion exactly four hundred years ago in the library of the King of Bohemia. Or merely to the trapped animal's unconscious feelings of respect for a well-made trap and a desire not to disappoint the person who went to so much trouble to set it . . .

My role is to see, describe and, now, write about what I saw. Someone or something is using me to untangle the tangled plot over whose direction I have as little influence as the pen has over the poets who wield it, or man over the gods who manipulate him, or the knife over the murderer. A plot whose denouement lies in your hands, Jorge.

Or should I say "in your tail".

*   *   *

This wasn't my first visit to Buenos Aires. When I was a child, I went with my Aunt Raquel to visit my Aunt Sofia and the Argentinian branch of the Vogelsteins. These two aunts brought me with them from Europe at the beginning of the Second World War. The third of the Vogelstein sisters, my mother, Miriam, stayed behind in Nazi Germany. She had a "protector" and so would come to no harm. Raquel set up home with me in Porto Alegre, where we had some poor relations; Sofia went to Buenos Aires, where we had some wealthy relations. Raquel used to say that they had drawn lots during the voyage, and the loser had got stuck with me. It wasn't true; of the two aunts, she was the most attached to me and would never have abandoned me. She proved an affectionate and devoted mother. In order to dedicate herself solely to me, she never married, and, in a sweetly sly way, she never let me marry either so as not to have to share her protectorate. It didn't take much persuasion to keep me single. I had always thought of a permanent domestic commitment to any woman other than Aunt Raquel as an intellectual threat. Not that another woman would steal my soul, but she would fatally interfere with the organisation of my books, for which Aunt Raquel had a reverential respect that she had transmitted to a long line of terrified cleaning ladies. The "young master's books" were not to be touched, wherever they were in our small Bonfim apartment, and the shelf containing my editions of Borges was a kind of reliquary which, if profaned, could cost them their hands.

In the end, before she asked to be sent to an old folks home, Aunt Raquel was obliged to be cared for by me, always cursing herself for putting me to so much bother. I should be devoting myself to my translations and to my books, not dealing out sedatives to a useless old woman. Going into a home was her way of freeing me from my gratitude and was yet another way of protecting me. Aunt Raquel protected me far too much throughout her life.

Perhaps she was afraid I might have inherited the fatal ingenuousness of her sister, Miriam, my mother, who died in a concentration camp in Poland, having been handed over to the Gestapo by her so-called "protector". Everything I know about my mother comes from my Aunt Raquel. Her red hair, her very white skin, her far too innocent heart. In the one photograph I have of her, the three Vogelstein sisters – Raquel, the oldest, Sofia, the second oldest, and Miriam, the youngest – can be seen sitting at the table of a sidewalk café on the Unter den Linden in Berlin, in the company of a man. My mother's "protector", according to Aunt Raquel. The monster about whom we never heard anything more. The four of them are smiling at the camera. My mother is the prettiest of the three sisters. She looks radiant in her summer dress and broad-brimmed hat. The man is wearing a woollen scarf around his neck and has one arm resting on the back of his chair. With the other, he is raising his glass to the photographer.

But that has nothing to do with our story, Jorge. All I remember of that visit with Aunt Raquel to Buenos Aires

– the first time the two sisters had met since fleeing Germany – was a fat cousin called Pipo, who had a high-pitched voice and kept kicking me.

Not until years later did I visit Buenos Aires again. Anxious to patch up our misunderstanding, Borges, I went (by bus!) in search of you. I was in my twenties at the time and, amongst other things, had done a few translations for *Mistério Magazine*, produced in Porto Alegre by the old Globo publishing house. The magazine printed translations of stories that appeared in *Ellery Queen's Mystery Magazine*, and, once, I translated a story by a certain Jorge Luis Borges, of whom I – an anglophile and americanophile already obsessed with Poe – had never heard. I thought the story was dreadful, confused and lacking in excitement. It wasn't clear at the end who the criminal was, and the reader was forced to draw his or her own conclusions. I decided to improve it. I added a few lugubrious Poe-like touches to the plot and a completely new surprise ending that belied everything that had gone before, including the author's account of events. Who would notice these changes in a translation into Portuguese of a translation into English of a story written in Spanish by an unknown Argentinian who should be grateful to me for adding a bit of extra blood and inventiveness to his text?

Your indignant but ironic letter did not take long to reach the publisher. Something about one mystery too many being on the loose in his magazine and which not even "Mr Queen" himself could explain. Some Brazilian bright spark, endowed with the most unbelievable arrogance, had been attacking defenceless texts and changing them out of all recognition. This was obviously a case for a committee of literary detectives or for a study of the criminal mind at work on fiction.

Since I was the criminal in question, I was charged with answering the letter. I tried to respond in the same tone saying that, far from seeing myself as a treacherous mutilator, I thought of myself more as a plastic surgeon undertaking minor corrective surgery, and I was very sorry that you did not appreciate the results of my poor attempts at cosmetic improvement. I apologised for having forgotten the first rule in plastic surgery which was to ask if the patient liked his new nose.

In your reply, Borges, you wrote that although you were accustomed to the arrogance of translators, I had clearly taken this occupational disease to new pathological heights. As a translator, I constituted quite enough of a danger, but as a plastic surgeon, I would be a positive public menace, since I displayed an alarming lack of anatomical precision. I had not tampered with the face of his text, I had added a grotesque tail, an ending that transformed the author into the worst villain a detective story can have: an unreliable narrator who conceals or falsifies information.

My "tail" did not even have the redeeming virtue of elegance. Or even of usefulness, which might have recommended it to an orangutan as a way of helping it to keep its balance, but not as a way of stripping someone else's text of all its original character. He requested that, in the future, I keep well away from both his texts and his nose.

By then, I had found out who Borges was, and my second letter was full of contrition and pleas for forgiveness. You did not respond to that second letter, nor to the third or the fourth. The fifth (in which I declared my growing remorse, my passionate conversion to your work, or to the few books of yours I had been able to find in Porto Alegre, and my intention of coming to Buenos Aires to meet you and apologise in person) was answered by a secretary, or your wife, or your mother, who wrote to say that Borges forgave me, but asked me, please, to leave him in peace. This only intensified both my remorse and my determination to come and see you.

I did everything possible to speak to you on that second visit to Buenos Aires. Without success. It was like walking round and round the outside of a labyrinth and never finding the way in. At your address in Calle Maipú or in the places where I knew I would be able to find you, I was told either that you were away or that you were ill or that you never ever received visitors, and that I should not insist. But I did. I asked for help from my relatives, to whom, after our visit to Buenos Aires, Aunt Raquel took to referring rather scornfully as "the Argentinian grandees", for although she was grateful to them for taking in Aunt Sofia, she clearly considered them our intellectual inferiors, unworthy of the cultural traditions of the Berlin Vogelsteins.

Fat Pipo, despite being only slightly older than me, was already an important figure in the financial world of Buenos Aires. He told me to leave everything in his hands. He would track down Borges and arrange for us to meet. Doubtless driven by remorse (for the way he had kicked me), he mobilised secretaries and influential acquaintances in order to fulfil his promise. Since the milieux in which Pipo and Borges lived were worlds apart, misunderstandings proliferated. One day, I found myself sitting in the bar in the Hotel Claridge with a little old man called Juan Carlos Borges, who was astonished at my interest in his work and at its success in Brazil, given that it had been years since he had published one of his brief botanical poems. I, of course, knew as soon as I saw him that Pipo had tracked down the wrong Borges. I didn't have the courage to disabuse the old man, however, and so I paid for his tea and toast and reaffirmed my devotion to his unjustly neglected work.

On another occasion, in the same Hotel Claridge, I found myself with a strange fellow called Borges Luis Jorge. He, at least, looked like you – to whom he referred as "an impostor" – but he wore dark glasses because, unlike you, he could see far too much. He had absolutely nothing to do with literature, which he abominated as "a waste of perception". His particular line was astronomy. He even told me that he was the only astronomer in the world who had dispensed with telescopes, because he could make out details on the Moon's surface with the naked eye. Borges Luis Jorge did not want tea, preferring a glass of cognac as compensation for his wasted time.

In the end, I gave up and returned to Porto Alegre, embittered by the failure of my penitential trip. I did not write to you for a long time after that. I only did so again when I sent, for your approval and possible use, a comparative study, in English, of your detective stories and Poe's Auguste Dupin stories which I had submitted to the editor of The Gold-Bug, who had duly returned it. You did not reply. The five or six letters that followed remained unanswered too, nor did you comment on the three "Borgian" stories, a mixture of plagiarism and hommage, which I also sent to you, having first failed to get them published. The grotesque "tail" had clearly not been forgotten.

*   *   *

My visit to the Israfel Society was, therefore, my third time in Buenos Aires. It was colder there than in Porto Alegre. The female conference steward at the airport had a mole right in the middle of her forehead and the name "Poe" written on her badge; I even thought at first that this was some miraculous coincidence, that she was the great-great-great-niece of some hitherto unsuspected Argentinian branch of the family which . . . But no, her name was written underneath in small letters. Angela. I have no experience of conferences. Indeed, I have no experience of anything very much. At least I didn't until I became enmeshed in this decidedly Borgian story. I was a dazzled, impressionable creature stepping off the plane and walking meekly into the trap, pleased to find a blonde angel welcoming me with her warm smile. I introduced myself, she consulted a list, said that the conference participants were staying at various hotels in the city and that my hotel was, was . . . Ah, yes, there I was. Señor Vogelstein from Brazil. In Calle Suipacha! An old hotel, but very good and recently refurbished. I had been destined for another hotel, away from the centre, but she herself had moved me to the one in Calle Suipacha, which was much better. And yes, yes, it was near Calle Maipú. It did not occur to me to ask why the name Vogelstein should have aroused Angela's instantaneous sympathy. And no-one seemed to know why the Israfel Society Conference, which normally alternated between Stockholm, Baltimore and Prague, in that order, had been suddenly shifted to Buenos Aires.

While Angela was filling out the vouchers that I had to hand to the taxi driver and to the hotel receptionist, I asked where Joachim Rotkopf was staying. She did not need to consult her list. She shook her head vigorously as if trying to drive the memory of Señor Rotkopf out through her ears. Señor Rotkopf had arrived that morning and had already made himself unforgettable. His disembarkation from the plane had proved problematic. He was over seventy, was travelling on his own, had difficulty walking and was full of complaints about the journey, the cold weather, the reception committee, everything. He had almost attacked a reporter, and Angela herself had overheard him hurling insults in mangled, Germanic Spanish.

Rotkopf lived in Mexico. In one of his letters to me, he said that he did not understand the modern lament that the conquest of Latin America had been a cultural violation. There had been no conquest, the natives had won, and their indolent, fatalistic culture still dominated the continent. They merely allowed the whites to think they were in charge in order to expose them to constant frustration and ridicule. "America is the defeat of Europe" was one of his phrases. There was only room in Latin America for defeated Europeans, like him, whose resignation passed for assimilation. He said that he lived in Mexico for the heat and because it was the best place in the world for talking to skulls and accustoming oneself to the idea of death.

Rotkopf's best-known and most controversial theory about Poe was that the American writer's work represented the final dissolution, into necrophilia and madness, of the Gothic imagination, the last gasp of European sensibility on the wild frontier, "before being eaten by the buffaloes". In the history of relations between Europe and the New World, it was hard to know who had violated whom. And out of that Gothic carcass, abandoned in America, was born European surrealism or the European response to the unconscious surrealism of the New World. For Rotkopf, the real Poe was the Poe translated by Baudelaire, the Poe rescued from the barbarians in order to revitalise the European vanguard. One of his last arguments with Professor Xavier Urquiza had been about precisely that and it had shaken the most recent conference of the Israfel Society, held in Stockholm. The two had traded insults during the talk given by the American, Oliver Johnson, whose subject was "Lovecraft and Poe, an obscure legacy".

In Stockholm, the Argentinian had called the German a racist and a Euromaniac; the German had accused him of philocretinism. Intellectual controversies tend to be like dog fights without the teeth, in which the barking not the biting does the damage. In the case of Rotkopf and Urquiza, however, according to the report in The Gold-Bug, they had very nearly come to bites. So much so that Oliver Johnson had to break off his discussion of Poe's influence on

Lovecraft – in which he defended the revolutionary theory that a supposed twentieth-century invention of Lovecraft's, the Necronomicon or book of dead names, was, in fact, an esoteric code dating back to the beginning of time and to which Poe had already made cryptic references – and leave the stage, with Rotkopf congratulating him, saying that every time an imbecile stopped talking, the intellectual climate on Earth improved slightly. Oliver Johnson had sworn to kill Joachim Rotkopf one day, and Rotkopf and Urquiza had continued their argument in the pages of The Gold-Bug, in a series of increasingly vitriolic articles, which I had followed with fascination, never dreaming that I would one day hear those magnificent, erudite dogs trading insults for real.

The three men would meet again in Buenos Aires, and now my smiling angel was telling me that Joachim Rotkopf would be staying at my hotel, in Calle Suipacha, despite his vociferous complaints that he had specifically asked for the Plaza. Then I discovered that Urquiza and Johnson would also be staying at the same hotel – and on the same floor as the German! This was almost more real life than I could have hoped for. The conference organisers clearly did not know what they were doing, or else knew all too well, and were part of the same conspiracy, of the same terrible stratagem of the Borges behind the Borges behind the conniving God who had snatched me from my safe, peaceful life in Bonfim.

Along with the vouchers and instructions on how to find a taxi and get to the hotel, Angela handed me the official conference programme and an invitation to the inaugural cocktail party at the Plaza. When I confessed that I had not brought a tie with me, she dazzled me with her smile (again!) and said that the stewards were prepared for all kinds of eccentric behaviour from participants, and that my lack of a tie was as nothing compared to what they could yet expect to see . . . Then she moved off, because another new arrival, a nervous Japanese man, required her attention. He was complaining about the fact that, for the first time in its history, the Israfel Society had broken with its tradition of holding conferences alternately in Stockholm, Baltimore and Prague, thus forcing him to alter all his plans and playing havoc with his vital fluids. I ended up sharing a taxi to the hotel with this same Japanese gentleman, who did not stop talking for an instant. He promised to protest vehemently to the board of the Israfel Society, if he could find them, for the Society's directors who organised the conferences never appeared in public.

Although the hotel rooms were small, they had very high ceilings, and the whole of one wall was filled by a floor-to-ceiling wardrobe with mirrored doors, so that the room appeared to be twice its actual size. I couldn't understand why my room was so ridiculously overheated. The cocktail party wasn't until the evening and the actual debates would begin the following morning, when Rotkopf's lecture would be the main event of the day. I hesitated, should I phone Aunt Sofia? If she found out that I had been in Buenos Aires and not been in touch with her, she would be hurt, but if I did contact her, that might make the "Argentinian grandees" feel obliged to invite me over, against my will and theirs. I decided to save them and myself the trouble. Twenty-five years on, fat Pipo would be even more unbearable, and even richer.

And what about Jorge Luis Borges? No, I wouldn't try to see you either. I had heard that you were very ill and no longer left the house. And I didn't want to inflict on myself the same sense of frustration I had experienced twenty-five years before. I would save you too, Jorge, from my presence in Buenos Aires.

I had no suitable clothes to wear to the cocktail party. I opted for wearing the same jacket I had worn on the flight, the only decent jacket I owned. When I passed through reception, on my way to the Plaza, I complained about my excessively hot room. I was told that the reason the heating in the hotel was on maximum was because of an emphatic demand from "Señor Rotkopf", in room 703, and because it was impossible to control the temperature in individual rooms. And, yes, Señores Oliver Johnson and Xavier Urquiza had also checked in, their rooms were 702 and 704 respectively. I arrived late at the cocktail party. I had decided to visit Calle Maipú first, rather than ignore it completely, even if it was only to see the door of your building. I may have sighed as I gazed at your door, but I really can't remember. I was resigned, master, to never meeting you.

At first, I recognised no-one in the grand salon in the Plaza, although I knew many of the Poe specialists from the pages of The Gold-Bug and from the photographs on the jackets of their books. They were my celebrities. I spotted Angela chatting to two men on the other side of the room and I went over to join her. She and her smile were like a sunny clearing in a forest of hostile tree trunks and threatening, talking lianas. One of the men was tall and thin, so tall that he had to stoop slightly in order to speak to Angela. He had a moustache, dark, slicked-back hair and the profile of a bird of prey. If he were to begin pecking at sweet Angela, he would have to start from the top of her head. The other man, with his back to me, looked much older and frailer. Angela recognised me and did not even need to consult my badge, which I wore around my neck instead of a tie, before introducing me. I was Vogelstein, from Brazil, and the old gentleman who was now turning to face me I would of course already know, it was the writer . . .

Jorge Luis Borges! I was standing next to Jorge Luis Borges! You were smiling at me and holding out your hand to be shaken. Your hand was real; yes, the hand of Jorge Luis Borges, which I was incredulously shaking, was made of flesh and blood! You were saying something, something about having been in Brazil the year before, about liking Brazil very much, about yourself being half-Brazilian. You were asking me where I was from in Brazil. What was my name again? I managed to return to Earth and say in a voice I had never heard before:

"Vogelstein. Vogelstein, from Porto Alegre."

And I added:

"Writer."

I examined your face, looking for some sign that my name had triggered a memory. Vogelstein, Borges! The one who wrote the letters, the stories, the translation in Mistério Magazine, the one who made up that insolent "tail"! You said:

"Vogelstein . . . We have some Vogelsteins in Buenos Aires. It's a Jewish name, isn't it?"

No! Not them, Borges, me! Not the rich philistines. I'm the Vogelstein from Porto Alegre. Your admirer and accidental collaborator, your colleague, albeit unpublished. Your . . . But you were introducing me to the other man.

"Have you two met? This gentleman is one of our principal Poe experts. Appropriately enough, he's a criminologist. Even more appropriately, his name is Cuervo, or Raven. I always tell Dr Raven here that his analyses of Poe's work are unfair to the author and to other analysts, since he is writing from the perspective of one of Poe's characters. He is speaking from within the work itself. He is a privileged observer!"

"Really, Jorge," said Cuervo, pretending to be annoyed.

This was apparently a favourite joke between you. Angela laughed and looked at me to see if I had understood the Spanish and the joke. I had learned Spanish so that I could read you in the original. I understand everything and I speak quite fluently, as you yourself remarked. I laughed more loudly than anyone, with a laugh I had never heard before either. I was high on my introduction to cosmopolitan life and on my proximity – at last! – to Borges. Pretty soon, I too would be calling you Jorge.

We spoke little during that first meeting. You told me that you were trying to dictate a book, *The Final Treatise on Mirrors*. I asked why "Final", and you replied that, at your age, it was reasonable to assume that everything you were doing was for the last time. I made various protesting noises and turned to take a glass of champagne from a passing tray, but just as I was raising my glass, desperately trying to think of some witty way of toasting your long life, I saw you being led off towards another group, towed along by a kidnapper in taffeta.

You were obviously the main attraction at the party, and the other foreigners present had only just realised you were there. I asked Cuervo about his friend's health. I think I said "Jorge's health". From on high, Cuervo pulled a face. Borges was not well. He had only agreed to come to the party as a kindness to him, for they were great friends. Expecting him to respond with laughter, I asked if it was true that the police occasionally consulted Borges, as an expert on cryptograms and enigmas and encoded clues, in order to solve a case. Cuervo, however, utterly straight-faced, said that, yes, they had often sought your advice when trying to solve certain complex cases, and that your contribution had always been most valuable, and that the two of you had frequent long conversations about detective fiction, Poe and criminology.

No, Cuervo himself was not a fiction writer. He said that he had no ambitions in that direction. He limited his writing to technical matters in his own field and to the fiction of Poe, but sometimes he combined the two interests. Once, for example, he had used the murder committed in the locked room from "The Murders in the Rue Morgue" in a class on forensic science and research. Of course! I remembered reading something about it in a special edition of The Gold-Bug, dedicated entirely to that one story by Poe, the first analytical detective story ever written, not counting Sophocles' Oedipus. Cuervo was a celebrity too! He told me that he contributed to the journal and occasionally took part in the conferences, but that he had no other links with that mysterious body, the Israfel Society. It was the first time I had heard the Society referred to as "mysterious". I didn't ask the reason.

Fortunately, Cuervo did not question me about my work and about what I was doing there, picking up a second glass of champagne before I had even finished my first. I would let it be understood that I too was a scholar, rather than a bedazzled conference neophyte, an intruder from Bonfim into real life. Another glass of champagne and I was likely to make some comment about Angela's décolletage and the mole between her breasts, which matched the one on her forehead. Something brilliant. It was possible that the night would end in witty talk, new theories – or even tangos – shared with Borges. Everything was possible in my new condition as man of the world. My cat Aleph had not died in vain.

You had disappeared into a crowd of admirers. I tried to convince myself that your remark about Cuervo's disloyalty to the author had been a veiled allusion to my translation of your story in the magazine, twenty-five years ago. Yes, Borges remembered me. Vogelstein. Vogelstein from Porto Alegre. You must remember!

A few glasses of champagne later, I was waiting for an opening that would allow me to get close to you again, when I spotted Joachim Rotkopf. He too was trying to reach you, but with none of my hesitancy. He approached like a cruiser, cutting a swathe through the other guests, brandishing his walking stick as he did so. He seemed irritated when I spoke to him, identifying myself as his correspondent from Porto Alegre. I was already rather drunk, but was nevertheless careful to hide my badge, for I had written to him using a pseudonym – Machado – and did not wish to have to explain the discrepancy. He, however, wasn't interested in me, whatever my name was. Yes, yes, we would talk later. We were staying in the same hotel? Excellent, excellent. We must have a drink together and talk, perhaps later that evening. And he continued his advance in your direction, carrying two ladies along with him and knocking over the Japanese gentleman with whom I had shared a taxi to the hotel.

It was in the midst of this crush of adoring fans, into which he had brutally elbowed his way, leaving me on the periphery, that the German provoked the first of the two scandals in which he would be involved at the Israfel Society Conference. He announced to you that he had come prepared to unmask your fellow Argentinian, Xavier Urquiza, to ruin his reputation and demolish him intellectually, at the same time pulverising the American, Oliver Johnson, whom he called "Lovecrafty", with documentary proof that his theory on the Necronomicon was not only utter nonsense, but plagiarised to boot. In response to your good-natured plea for peace amongst intellectuals, he added that he would also have a few things to say about the intellectual dishonesty of certain "fake Europeans" like yourself, Borges, a remark that elicited indignant murmurs all round.

Rotkopf was as tall as Cuervo, who was not on hand to defend his frail friend, and so you merely smiled timidly at the German's rudeness. I was surprised at how tall he was and at the redness of his skin, which contrasted with his very white hair. In one of his letters he had told me that he had been born in the ideal land, Germany, where all intellectuals should be born, but beneath the wrong sun. The solar culture of the Mexicans was a recognition that they would never have an idea more valuable to worship than the Sun, and that the Sun made up for their lack of a Goethe. It was the Sun that had taken him to Mexico. And even there, he kept the heating on in his Mexican home all year round. He moved awkwardly and yet had the lean body of an ex-athlete.

The lady in taffeta, who had not relinquished your arm for an instant, decided to put an end to the incident. She removed her prey from the unpleasant German and headed off in the direction of the buffet, with the supportive crush of admirers acting as a rearguard.

The second scandal provoked by Joachim Rotkopf at the conference was, of course, his murder that same night.

Angela did not understand my remark about her legs when we encountered one another again before a ruined pyramid of prawns. This did not surprise me. I myself did not know what I was saying. After all that champagne, I was in no condition to understand my own Spanish. She was asking me if I would mind going back to the hotel with Rotkopf, since no-one else wanted to travel in the same car as him. In his search for someone who could put up with him for more than two minutes, Rotkopf had managed to knock over a tray of canapés, another female conference steward and the same Japanese gentleman whom he had knocked over before, who had immediately left the party in high dudgeon. Xavier Urquiza and Oliver Johnson had, very wisely, avoided any confrontation with Rotkopf. This, however, had not prevented the German, when he recognised the American, who had the build and complexion of a maharajah, from chanting grotesquely:

"Israfel, Israfel, does it ring a bell?"

Apart from Johnson and myself, no-one understood the meaning of this improvised jingle, sung in a falsetto voice by Rotkopf, while he beat time with his walking stick. In one of his letters, he had told me how he had poked fun at Johnson's mania for discovering hidden meanings in everything by sending him, anonymously, an interpretation of Poe's poem about the angel Israfel. He claimed that if the poem was read in a mirror, it would reveal a kabbalistic code. Johnson had been so thrilled by the discovery that he had quoted it in one of his articles. He had then received a sarcastic note from Rotkopf, identifying himself as the author of the false information and advising Johnson to check his sources more carefully. Rotkopf had taken great satisfaction in telling me about this cruel practical joke.

As I trailed after you and your entourage, Jorge, until Cuervo managed to wrest you from the lady in taffeta and take you home, I heard various suggestions about what should be done to the unfortunate German, and none of them was charitable. A rumour had gone round that when old Urquiza found out what Rotkopf had said about him and about Borges, he had decided to challenge Rotkopf to a duel. According to another rumour, one of Urquiza's sons, an athletic young man with a foolish face, who was present at the party, had to be restrained from attacking the German there and then. And Johnson, fleeing any contact with Rotkopf, had repeated his promise to kill him as soon as he got the chance.

In the car, alone with me and the driver, Rotkopf seemed unaware of the stir he had caused. He joked with the driver, asking if he was a *porteño*, a native of Buenos Aires, and if he too believed that Buenos Aires, that "simulation", really was a European city, and if, like all *porteños*, he considered himself to be "that physiological impossibility", a sub-equatorial Briton. The driver was not amused. By the look in his eyes when we got out of the car, it seemed to me that he too would gladly have seized the first opportunity to kill the German. The wind began blowing hard just as we were getting out of the taxi, and we had to battle our way across the pavement to the door of the hotel.

Rotkopf suggested that we adjourn to his room and have a drink to warm us up. Since he could not bring the Sun with him, he had brought some tequila instead. In the elevator, he appeared to look at me for the first time. So I was Machado, from where exactly? Ah, yes, Porto Alegre. He had imagined me to be younger, my letters had struck him sometimes as extremely youthful in their enthusiasm and ingenuousness and in their obsessive curiosity. Why had I wanted to know so much about his life? Why had I asked about his work as a cryptographer during the Second World War, when that had so little bearing on our mutual interest in Poe? Surely I did not subscribe to the school of thought, which had reached its absurd apogee in Johnson, that found coded meanings in everything Poe had written. I did not seem quite that stupid. He wasn't insulting me. At least not intentionally. In the corridor, he again sang the jingle with which he had taunted poor Johnson, "Israfel, Israfel, does it ring a bell?", and let out a thunderous guffaw. When we went into his room, I noticed that the door of room 701 was ajar and that someone was watching us.

Our conversation, or what I remember of it, was almost pleasant, despite the overheated room, the wind rattling the windows and the hot tequila after so much champagne. Before I left him, I said, in all sincerity, that I thought his life was in danger. I advised him to lock the door of his room and put the chain on, so that it could not even be opened with the master key. He appeared to ignore me, but as soon as I left, I heard the sound of the door being locked and the chain being put on.

29

My immediate concern then was remembering where my room was. What with cocktail parties, a meeting with Jorge Luis Borges, the imminence of intellectual battles and possible physical violence, and with me in the thick of it all, my head was spinning. Aunt Raquel had shielded me too much. Real life had rushed in upon me, and this instantaneous cosmopolitanism was disorienting, it was all so new and intoxicating. Plus the champagne and the hot tequila.

When I went downstairs to find out where my room was (it was room 202), and to collect my key from reception, Xavier Urquiza and Oliver Johnson, also buffeted by the wind, were just coming into the hotel. They arrived at the same time, but not together, for they too hated each other. The American found a pretext not to join the Argentinian in the elevator up to the same fateful seventh floor as Joachim Rotkopf. I took the stairs to my room on the second floor. I did so quickly and effortlessly, for I could no longer feel my legs.

I was woken in the middle of the night by the phone ringing. The sound of Joachim Rotkopf's voice as if speaking under water. Bubbling, as if it were emerging from his throat along with some liquid. A single word, which I did not understand. Then silence. I noticed that the wind had dropped.

I went up to the seventh floor and knocked on the door of room 703. No movement, no noise. I knocked more

30

loudly. I saw the door of 701 inch open, but no-one came out. I banged on Rotkopf's door again, this time with the palm of my hand. Nothing. I went down to the hotel reception. The night porter could only have been about twenty at most. It was even more difficult trying to persuade him to break down the door of room 703 than it had been waking him up. He couldn't help, he was alone in reception, he needed authorisation from the manager, from the gentleman . . . There's no time, I yelled, dragging him over to the elevator. We might be able to prevent someone from dying. "¡Vámonos!" I had just managed to get him into the elevator, when he realised that he would have to go back and fetch the master key, which took him an age to find.

The key was no use anyway, since the door was locked from the inside. We had to break it down. I went in and found Joachim Rotkopf lying on the floor on his side, still dressed as he had been when I left him hours before. His body was in a strange position, bent at the waist, with his legs straight and his arms outstretched above his head, forming an open V. The telephone was on the floor, with the receiver, off the hook, lying beside his head. I did not let the night porter come into the room with me, so that he would not see the blood on the floor. The poor lad was terrified enough as it was.

"Go and get help!" I shouted. "Call a doctor. Call the manager!"

Neither the doctor, nor the manager, nor any of the other

sleepy hotel staff who invaded the room, summoned by the night porter, could help Joachim Rotkopf, nor were they of much help to the police, for by the time the police had arrived, everything in the room had been moved, including the dead man's body. The police only managed to reconstruct the scene thanks to my statement – as precise as my feelings of shock and the amount of alcohol in my blood at the time allowed – detailing what I had seen when I examined the room after the night porter had rushed off to get assistance. How had the body been lying when I found it? I had to rack my brains to remember. It had formed the letter V, of that I was sure. But as to its position . . . The body was lying with its bottom, or the vertex of the V, against the mirrors covering one wall of the room. That was right, with its bottom against the mirror. The blood had formed a pool on the carpet, and he had dragged himself or been dragged across it to the mirror. The bottle of tequila and the glasses we had used were still in the same place, on a table, but beside the bottle there were four playing cards that had not been there before. There was no sign of the weapon that had been used to cut Joachim Rotkopf's throat and then been plunged twice into his stomach.

Amongst the hotel guests who came to gawk at the scene of the crime and complicate the work of the police still further, I saw neither Oliver Johnson nor Xavier Urquiza. They did not open the doors of their rooms. The guest in 701 opened his just a crack, but, again, did not appear.

X

THE CONFERENCE WAS CANCELLED, JOACHIM ROTKOPF'S violent death had shocked everyone, including you – but you could not quite manage to conceal your pleasure. You could not keep your mouth in the correct expression of grief and concern. A conference on Edgar Allan Poe interrupted by a murder committed in a locked room, it was like a story by Poe himself! It was regrettable, but it was fantastic too. Several times during our conversation, when I went to visit you that evening after the crime, a flicker of joy ran across your face, like a child escaping the control of a stern father, until brought to heel again. I knew you would be pleased, Jorge.

There was no disguising my own joy. I hadn't slept. I was still stunned by what I had seen in Rotkopf's hotel room, by the questions asked by the police and, later, by reporters, by a vertiginous morning during which only the gentle presence of Angela saved me from nervous collapse. Angela had even held my head, as Aunt Raquel used to do, while I vomited up everything I had drunk the night before. But now I was in Jorge Luis Borges' library. I had reached the heart of the labyrinth and the monster had offered me a choice of tea, maté or sherry. I was sitting there amongst your books, beneath your Piranesi engravings, drinking your doubtless English tea, and you were listening to me, and this time it wasn't a dream. Sorrow and delight were battling for possession of your face, just as nausea and ecstasy were battling for dominion over my stomach.

We were sitting in battered leather armchairs (exactly as in my dreams), in a triangle around an electric heater. Cuervo had taken me to your presence so that I could describe to you what I had seen in the dead man's room after the door had been broken down. First, he summarised what the police knew. The death had been caused by three knife wounds, two in the belly and one in the throat. Wounds inflicted by a hypothetical knife, for no knife had yet been found. The exact time of the murder – difficult to say. Something about the excessive heat in the room interfering with the coagulation of the blood. Rotkopf was still alive fifteen minutes before he was found, when he phoned me at three in the morning, but he could have been stabbed at any time after I left his room at around eleven. The door was locked from the inside; the chain had been on, too, and had snapped when we broke down the door. The windows were locked from the inside as well. There was no window in the bathroom. A door connecting 703 with 704 – Xavier Urquiza's room – was also locked, and the key had not left the drawer in the hotel manager's desk.

"What did he say to you on the phone?" you asked.

"I couldn't quite understand, what with his German accent and the cut to his throat . . . It sounded like 'Djebrrokee'."

"Cherokee?"

"It could have been."

"The Cherokees. The only one of the great American tribes to have a syllabic alphabet . . ."

Cuervo and I exchanged glances. If this information had provoked a chain of deductive reasoning – the slit throat as some kind of bungled attempt at scalping – you obviously very swiftly considered it and dismissed it, for you made a gesture, brushing away the thought as if it were a fly. You asked me to go on. What position was the body in when I entered the room?

"It was lying in a V shape."

You made a noise that could have been the beginning of an immediately aborted laugh. The expression on your face was one of extreme satisfaction, as if you yourself had thought up the idea.

"A V?!"

"Yes, a letter V, like this."

Forgetting that you couldn't see me, I imitated as best I could the highly unnatural position in which I had found the dead man: lying on his side, bent at the waist and with arms and legs stretched out straight. Cuervo described my clumsy pantomime to you. I added that, if I remembered rightly, the vertex of the V was resting against the mirror. I don't know if I used the word "backside", but you understood. His backside was pressed against the mirror, with his legs pointing in one direction and his arms in the other. You asked:

"What do you mean, 'if I remember rightly'?"

I explained that I couldn't be sure. That I was in an agitated state, dazed with sleep and still slightly drunk. That I had never seen a dead person before, or so much blood. I couldn't be sure.

You asked about the blood.

The blood had left a long trail across the floor, like a red sheet. Rotkopf had been dragged over to the mirror, or had dragged himself over there. Cuervo said it was impossible to know. By the time the police arrived, a lot of people had already been into the room. Quite absurdly, someone had even tried to revive the dead man with heart massage. There were bloody footprints everywhere. My shoes were stained with blood too. What else had I seen in the room? I told you about the cards on the table.

There were three cards, forming a broken fan. Two cards,

a space, and then the other card. The cards, according to Cuervo, had disappeared. No-one else had seen them. What cards were they?

"The 10 of clubs and the jack of spades together and the king of hearts on its own."

I saw from your faces that, given my supposed state of shock on discovering the body, such exactitude surprised you both. I added:

"I think."

"Had you and he been playing cards in the room?" asked Cuervo.

"No. We just talked and drank. I didn't even see a pack of cards."

I had used the wrong word in Spanish — *barajo*. You corrected me:

"*Baraja*."

"I didn't see a . . ."

I stopped because you had held up your hand, calling for silence. You were thinking. Another satisfied smile was evading control and taking shape on your lips.

You said:

"Jabberwocky."

"What?"

"The word Rotkopf said to you on the phone. Wasn't it 'Jabberwocky'?"

"It might have been . . ."

"There's a story over there somewhere . . ." you indicated one of the shelves in your library, "in which a dead man is found . . ."

". . . pointing to a passage from Lewis Carroll's poem 'Jabberwocky', in *Alice Through the Looking Glass*," I said, completing his thought and taking special care over my English pronunciation, so as to impress him. "The poem contains a clue to the murderer's name."

"Exactly."

"I myself wrote a story in which the murder victim is found pointing at the line 'as if from beyond the looking glass' from your poem 'Edgar Allan Poe', Borges, and which leads to the solution of the crime," I told him.

It was one of the three stories I had sent to you and which had vanished into your silence. In my story, the initials of Edgar Allan Poe seen through the looking glass formed the word "pae", and the father, or "pa", was the murderer. And as an epigraph to the story I had used your remark about paternity and mirrors being equally abominable because both increased the number of men. But you appeared not to hear me. You said:

"Rotkopf didn't have a copy of Carroll's book to hand and so he said the name of the poem. 'Jabberwocky'."

"Should we look for a clue in the poem, then?" asked Cuervo.

You gestured vaguely in my direction.

"Perhaps Señor . . ."

You had forgotten my name!

"Vogelstein," prompted Cuervo.

"Perhaps Vogelstein would be so kind as to find the book for us. I have a beautiful edition of Carroll's complete works, I think it's somewhere here . . ."

Your hand drifted up towards one of the shelves. I had already got up to look for the book, but you went on:

"Unless, of course, our friend Rotkopf was trying to give us a different message . . ."

"What?" asked Cuervo.

"In the story of Alice, the poem is written in a strange language, which she cannot decipher. When she realises that she is on the other side of the looking glass and that everything is, therefore, back to front, Alice places the book in front of a mirror, just as the unfortunate Dr Rotkopf did with his own body, then everything becomes clear. She can read the poem."

"Should we then read the clues backwards?"

"Our only clues are the body forming a V and the cards."

"And a V with the vertex pressed against the mirror," you said, "is an X."

"For Xavier," said Cuervo.

We sat in silence for a few seconds. Then you made a resigned gesture with your hands and said:

"There you are. The name of the murderer. One should not multiply mysteries."

"They should be simple," went on Cuervo. "Remember Poe's stolen letter, remember Zangwill's locked room."

"Or complex," I said, completing the quotation. "Remember the Universe."

You smiled.

"I see you have read my stories, Señor Vogelstein."

I almost said: "And I see you have not read mine, Señor Borges," but this was not the moment for resentment. I said: "Both prose and poetry, Señor Borges." Ecstasy, or possibly the tea, had overcome my feelings of nausea. My stomach was now a centre radiating a warm sense of well-being, like the heater around which we were sitting. This warmth increased a few more degrees when you said:

"Call me Jorge."

Cuervo was standing up. He would have to take a closer look at the connecting door between rooms 703 and 704. He would also have to consider the most diplomatic way of detaining Dr Xavier Maldonado de Llentes y Urquiza in Buenos Aires and inviting him to make a statement before he returned to his estate in Mendoza. Urquiza was a difficult and controversial figure. You said that you had never understood what a bigoted, Catholic, aristocratic landowner was doing concocting theories about Edgar Allan Poe. He was the Israfel Society's Argentinian representative. It was said that his library was one of the largest in the country. You and he got on well, although you rarely met and, when you did, you always avoided speaking about a certain person. Who? God. According to Urquiza, the entire work of the atheist Borges was "a theology in search of a centre".

"I just wish the dead man had simply told you the name of the murderer over the phone, instead of making such a complicated game out of it," said Cuervo.

"That's because you're not a writer of fiction, Cuervo," you said. "Señor Vogelstein and I are only sorry that the game has proved so easy. We still had many brilliant literary speculations up our sleeves."

Señor Vogelstein and I! You had included me in your rapid deductions and had described me as an equal. We were a double act – writers and decipherers of universes, simple and complex. Borges and I, I and Borges. I had been accepted! You perhaps even remembered the translation I did for *Mistério Magazine*, our exchange of correspondence, my unanswered letters, my insistence on seeing you, my three stories . . . You knew who I was from the moment Angela introduced us at the cocktail party and were merely playing with my anxiety, merely postponing the revelation that you had recognised me and that you accepted me. You were merely pretending that you had forgotten my name. You too were playing a game with me, Jorge. Weren't you?

My happiness did not, apparently, show on my face, for Cuervo remarked that I looked absolutely dreadful and should try and get some sleep. He would take me back to the hotel. Before we said goodbye, I glanced again around that library in which I had so often imagined myself. Only one thing did not match my dream: I had not expected to see so many books not on the shelves, but arranged in piles on tables and on the floor. I remarked on the number of books, and you said that many of them had belonged to your father.

"He said that the number of books he owned was the only kind of wealth he had in common with the King of Bohemia. I never really understood what he meant, but that didn't stop me feeling like the heir to the King of Bohemia in this library. In my researches for my *Final Treatise on Mirrors*, I stumbled upon the experiments carried out in the library of Rudolf II, in which reading texts in mirrors was commonplace, and so I feel perfectly at home. This library is a modest branch of the royal library of Prague, if that still exists. But Urquiza's library is even bigger."

I examined the Piranesi engravings on the wall and told you that I too admired those meticulously drawn imaginary ruins.

"To live is to leave ruins," I quoted.

"Who said that?" you asked.

"Walter Benjamin, in an essay about Poe."

As we were leaving the library, you said:

"And what about the cards? The 10, the jack and the king?"

Cuervo shrugged and said:

"Think about it while we talk to Dr Xavier Urquiza."

"I've just remembered something!" I said.

"What?"

"About the cards. Someone had made holes in the jack's eyes."

Joy finally escaped all the controls and spread over your face, Jorge.

* * *

"Traces."

That was the first thing you said when we went back to your library later that evening.

"I'm sorry?"

"To live means to leave traces, not ruins. Walter Benjamin."

You were sitting in the same armchair. A remnant of July sun was still coming in through the window, but the library was in darkness. Cuervo suggested turning on a light.

"If it is any point requiring reflection . . ." you began.

Cuervo and I continued the quotation from Poe in unison, he in Spanish and I in English:

". . . we shall examine it to better purpose in the dark."

We all laughed.

"'The Gold-Bug'," I said.

Cuervo was shocked by my mistake, since I had been so quick to identify Auguste Dupin's words. You were merely intrigued.

"No, no," said Cuervo. "'The Purloined Letter'."

"Of course. It's just that for some reason 'The Gold-Bug' strikes me as more pertinent to this case."

You were still pondering. Cuervo, feeling restless, had not yet sat down. We had come back to your library because investigations at the hotel had proved frustrating. While I was asleep in my room, Cuervo and his men had been testing out all the hypotheses suggested by the clue the dead man had left. That is, if the X referred to Xavier Urquiza. Even if Urquiza had somehow got access to the key to the door that connected his room to Rotkopf's — a door that was only ever used if someone occupied both rooms and needed to be able to come and go between them — it had clearly not been opened in the last six months. The hotel had undergone a recent refurbishment, which had included repainting. The space between the door and the frame had been painted over. The paint was intact.

"Wait," I said. "In Poe's locked room story, 'The Big Bow Mystery', the murderer . . ."

I had again shocked Cuervo, this time by confusing Poe's story with that of Zangwill — doubtless the effects of the previous night.

"You mean in 'The Murders in the Rue Morgue', by Poe . . ."

"Yes, yes, of course. In Poe's story the murderer is an orangutan that climbs in through the window. When it leaves the same way, the window closes behind it so that it looks as if the window latch had returned to its original position, but . . ."

"I examined the windows carefully," said Cuervo impatiently. "Don't forget I wrote a thesis on 'The Murders in the Rue Morgue'. The windows were securely closed from the inside."

You were laughing at us.

"What I would like to know," you said, "is if you gentlemen seriously believe that an orangutan – a last-minute recruit rapidly trained up by Dr Xavier – could have scaled the outside of the hotel all the way up to the seventh floor, with a dagger clenched between its teeth . . ."

"Don't forget, my dear Borges, it's an old building with a heavily decorated façade that would prove perfectly scaleable, and that Dr Xavier has a son who not only looks like an orangutan, but, living as he does in Mendoza, at the foot of the Andes, is also an experienced climber. In fact, people say that climbing, both real and social, is all he does in life, much to his father's disgust. Intellectuals often have idiotic children. In this case, however, we're dealing with an innocent idiot. After the cocktail party at the Plaza, he dined with friends, then went on to a nightclub, and that was where he was, surrounded by equally idiotic witnesses, at the presumed time of the murder."

"Did you manage to speak to Xavier Urquiza?" you asked.

"Yes. Dr Xavier expressed sincere joy at the German's death, his only regret being that they had neglected to tear out his heart, as in an Aztec ritual, although he admitted that it might have been difficult to find a heart to tear out."

Xavier Urquiza had told Cuervo that he had slept heavily and had heard no noises coming from the room next door, either of a murder taking place or of a door being broken down; he had heard no commotion either in the corridor or in the room when the body was found. There was nothing compromising in Urquiza's room, although Cuervo had only examined it superficially while they were talking. There were no traces of blood on the floor or anywhere else, and there was nothing in Urquiza's behaviour to indicate that he was feeling tense or trying to hide something. Nothing.

The X had led us nowhere.

There was almost total darkness in the library now. Cuervo was pacing up and down, whether in search of a lamp to turn on or because this was his way of thinking, I don't know.

"Let's not abandon the X so soon," you said. "What else could it mean?"

"In mathematics, it symbolises an unknown or variable quantity," suggested Cuervo.

"Victor Hugo said that the X signified crossed swords, a battle with an uncertain result, which is why it symbolised destiny for philosophers and the unknown for mathematicians," was my contribution.

Cuervo:

"It could mean the cross or Christ . . ."

You:

"Sir Thomas Browne, that magnificent seventeenth-century madman and one of my favourite authors . . ."

"And the author, as it happens, of the text that Poe uses as an epigraph for 'The Murders in the Rue Morgue'," said Cuervo.

"And which, in turn, is a translation of a passage from the life of the Emperor Tiberius written in Latin by Suetonius. . . ." I added, thus concluding our erudite little minuet to the satisfaction of all.

"Sir Thomas Browne wrote a treatise on the X, which he saw as the union of temporal knowledge and magical knowledge, with one pyramid facing downwards and one facing upwards," you went on. "It is also the duplication of the V, the Roman letter with the most potent mystical charge, for it represents the five human senses and is, at the same time, shape, letter and number, or geometry, writing and mathematics, the three means at our disposal for interpreting the world. But we had better not head off down that dark path. Anyway, I've just remembered that Poe wrote a story in which the X replaces the O, entitled . . ."

"'X-ing the Paragrab'!" Cuervo and I said, again in unison.

Of course! In Poe's story, a newspaper editor with a mania for using the letter O in his texts discovers that, because the letter O is missing from the newspaper's typecase, it has been replaced by an X in one of his articles, to the great perplexity of his readers and the delight of his enemies. The X formed by Rotkopf's V-shaped body with the vertex positioned against the mirror would, in that case, represent an O.

"It isn't easy to make an O with the body, or a C that can be transformed into an O with the help of the mirror. But any reader of Poe would realise that X could mean O," I said. "And it would be only natural for a cryptographer like Rotkopf to substitute one letter for another."

"Was Rotkopf a cryptographer?" you asked.

"Yes, during the war. I don't know on which side, though."

And I told him the little I had gleaned of the German's biography from his letters.

"Right, then, so instead of an X we have an O," said Cuervo.

With an admirable sense of the dramatic, someone turned on a light in the library just a second before you said:

"O for Oliver."

Oliver Johnson had more than once declared his intention of killing Joachim Rotkopf. He was staying in the room next to his in the hotel, and although he was now in his sixties and possessed an opulent paunch, he seemed otherwise in good physical shape. And he certainly hated Rotkopf enough to enter his enemy's room, plunge a knife once into his throat and twice into his belly and then leave. But enter and leave how? That was something only the murderer could reveal, in the fullness of time. Cuervo appeared unhappy at the prospect of interrogating the American as a suspect, based only on a hypothetical X that was actually meant to be an O. The dead man was becoming far too cryptic for Cuervo's taste. Why didn't he speak clearly? It struck him as unreasonable that a man, while bleeding to death, should stage this detailed accusatory tableau, trusting in the deductive powers of readers of Poe.

"We're not being very scientific about this," he protested.

He would, nevertheless, talk to Johnson and examine his room.

"Were there any signs that Rotkopf's room had been searched — open drawers, papers in disarray?"

Your question was addressed to me.

"Not that I noticed," I replied. "But then I didn't really look. I was too shocked by the sight of the body and the blood . . ."

"By the time the police arrived, the whole room had been turned upside down," said Cuervo, interrupting me. "Even the body had been moved. Why do you ask?"

"I heard Rotkopf say at the cocktail reception that he had proof that Johnson's theory about Poe and Lovecraft was both absurd and a plagiarism," you said. "Johnson wanted to stop Rotkopf giving his lecture and presenting those proofs today. He killed Rotkopf and vanished with the proof. There's your motive. Intellectual pride under threat. Far more convincing than mere dislike, especially bearing in mind that we're dealing here with academics. Vogelstein, did Rotkopf show you any document that he was proposing to use today against Johnson?"

"No. He just said that he was going to reveal to the world the trick he had played on Johnson."

And I told them how Rotkopf had invented a kabbalistic interpretation of the poem "Israfel" when read in a mirror, which Johnson had taken to be true. Both you and Cuervo remembered the embarrassing scene in the middle of the reception room in the Plaza Hotel when the tall German had brandished his walking stick and sung "Israfel, Israfel, does it ring a bell?" to Johnson.

"An eminently knifeable man, that Rotkopf," you remarked.

Cuervo was heading for the door, clearly unhappy about the mission that awaited him.

"Dr Johnson will be invited to make a statement. I can foresee diplomatic complications. Are you coming?"

Cuervo was talking to me, but you were the one who answered.

"Señor Vogelstein is staying here. I think I might be able to interest him in a bowl of hot soup and some dry crackers."

And Cuervo departed, leaving me alone with you, in paradise.

I REMEMBER EVERYTHING WE SAID THAT NIGHT. EXACTLY.

Me:

"O. The mother of all vowels. Symbol of God. That which has neither beginning nor end."

You:

"A snake eternally biting its own tail. Symbol of Eternity."

Me:

"Its origin is the semitic word *ayin*, which in Phoenician means 'eye'."

You:

"I disagree. It must be a pictogram of the Sun. The symbol of the pharaoh Akhenaten, who was the first to conceive of god as 'author' of the Universe, and consequently of the author as god. Our patron saint, Vogelstein."

Me:

"You said somewhere that you would like to write in one of the Nordic languages because they have more vowels, and vowels are more serious."

You:

"Did I say that? But Latin languages have more vowels than Nordic ones! I think what I meant was that I would like to write in one of those ancient northern tongues which were almost entirely made up of vowels. I've always felt it had something to do with the climate. They were hot languages, insulated by all those heaped up vowels."

Me:

"Ancient Hebrew only had consonants. Presumably so that there was no risk of them accidentally writing the secret name of God."

You:

"Or perhaps that was to do with the climate too. Consonants were more open and airy, more suited to a language of the desert."

"You also said that you hated sans serif typefaces."

"Oh, yes, they're terrible! All those naked letters, reduced to their stark scaffolding. No-one can possibly recognise their mother tongue when printed in a Futura typeface. It lacks maternal warmth, it lacks friendliness."

"I fear Cuervo may be right: we are somewhat unscientific."

"And prejudiced too. Vowels can be dispensed with. A text written solely using vowels would be illegible, but in a text using only consonants, one could guess the vowels.

A text in which an X replaced all the Os, as in that story by Poe, might prove difficult to read, but would, ultimately, be decipherable."

"The fact that E is the most common letter in the English language is the key to deciphering the code in the parchment in Poe's story 'The Gold-Bug' . . ."

"Yes, I was curious to know why you said to Cuervo that 'The Gold Bug' was more pertinent to the case."

Before I could reply, the soup and crackers arrived, served to us in our armchairs by a woman all in black and with a very Indian face, so we moved on to the silent task of eating and balancing plates, which you did rather more skilfully than I. Then, and for what remained of that magical evening, we talked about Oliver Johnson, about his theories and about the *Necronomicon*, the book of dead names. It was time to set off down that dark road. I remember it all.

We each knew a little about Johnson's theories and about his conjectures on H.P. Lovecraft, Poe and occultism. Beginning with *The Nameless City*, first published in 1921, and throughout most of his strange œuvre, the American writer Lovecraft makes repeated references to a mysterious book, originally called *Al Azif* and written in Damascus in the first century A.D. by a presumably mad poet, Abdul Alhazred or El Hazzared. In order to establish its authenticity, Lovecraft had provided a chronological history and even a pseudobibliography of the book, which had been translated into Greek with the title *Necronomicon* and subsequently into Latin, before its prohibition by Pope Gregory IX in 1232. There was a German edition in 1440, a Greek edition published in Italy between 1500 and 1550, and an English translation made by John Dee around 1600, which was the one cited by Lovecraft. The banned book, based on hallucinations induced by a particular alkaloid herb ingested by the mad poet, was said to contain the names of all the Evil beings who had dominated Earth before the advent of Man – the dead names, whose evocation and reproduction in writing would threaten Humanity.

You:

"It was always thought that the *Necronomicon* was pure invention on the part of Lovecraft, who, like Poe, loved mysterious stories full of bogus erudite allusions to obscure rites."

Me:

"Like Borges too."

You, pretending that you hadn't heard me:

"It was even thought that the name of the mad poet, Alhazred, our 'El Hazzared', was a joking reference on Lovecraft's part to 'Hazzard', one of his family names."

Me:

"Then Johnson began to notice curious similarities between the *Necronomicon* and other books of occultist philosophy, from the hermetic tradition of Egyptian freemasonry and from even further back in time, and to realise that Lovecraft himself doubted the originality of his own creation."

"In other words, Lovecraft wasn't inventing anything. He had intuited a truth and unwittingly revealed it."

"Or had invented the truth."

"In Stockholm last year, in the paper that Johnson didn't get to read because Rotkopf and Urquiza wouldn't let him speak, but which he published later on, Johnson suggested that Lovecraft had discovered that he had been the involuntary instrument of a revelation. Lovecraft was convinced that the Necronomicon was real, that it actually existed, and that Poe had known about it too. Or that Poe had also been used by hidden beings to reveal themselves in words."

"Because Poe, according to Lovecraft, according to Johnson, was also in the habit of ingesting the same alkaloid herb that had helped Lovecraft understand the mad poet's prose. And his work was full of veiled references to those terrible dead names."

"The identification of Lovecraft with Poe wasn't due solely to the fact that both were from New England, a land of witchcraft and gloomy valleys, the only American equivalent to the dark forests of Europe. Both men used the same esoteric code, or had, by chance, stumbled on the same code and uncovered a nest of hidden meanings."

"Lovecraft could, of course, have been inventing that secret link with Poe, whom he admired and even imitated."

"Or Johnson could have had actual proof that the two men were interpreters, whether voluntary or involuntary,

of the same coded language, something that would revo-
lutionise the study of Poe's work."

"A proof that Rotkopf would have undermined had he
not been murdered."

"But undermined how?"

"Quite. If we knew that, we would know the motive for
the crime. Let's just hope that Cuervo is, at this very
moment, scientifically tracking down either the document
that the murderer did not want Rotkopf to read out today,
or Johnson's document that Rotkopf was intending to
undermine. Although I suspect . . ."

You stopped speaking. We were both bent forwards in our
ancient leather armchairs, and the electric heater was
purring at our feet like an accomplice. Jorge and I, the hot-
footed conspirators. The only lamp cast a dim circle of light
that just barely illuminated us and left the rest of the library
in darkness. You made an episcopal gesture with hands
open, taking in the invisible shelves around us, before
finishing your sentence:

". . . that the solution lies here. Solutions can always be
found in libraries."

Dr John Dee, to whom Lovecraft attributed the translation
of his apocryphal book, had really existed. He was an
English magus and cosmographer, astrologer to Queen
Elizabeth I, and one of the first to examine with something approaching scientific method the existence of

parallel universes and of mysterious forces that seek expression in the written word.

"The written word, Vogelstein," you said, still holding your hands out to the surrounding shelves. "The powerful word into which everything must be transformed if it is to be invoked and brought into existence. And which any system, natural or supernatural, logical or magical, needs in order to have a history, because one must write in order to remember and to understand, or in order to foresee and to control. And which you and I manipulate with no special licence, often like innocent children playing with loaded pistols."

"Or sharpened knives."

"Or murderous knives. We have a gift for placing one word after another coherently and creatively, but we could unwittingly be serving a coherence entirely unknown to us and thus inventing terrifying truths. We write in order to remember, but those memories might belong to other people. We could be creating universes, like Akhenaten's god, merely to amuse ourselves. We might unwittingly be placing monsters in the world. And without even leaving our chairs."

"Wasn't Dr John Dee a member of the court of Rudolf II in Prague?"

"Yes, he was!"

You were thrilled to discover that I knew about Rudolf II, King of Bohemia, another magnificent madman from the sixteenth century, who employed a full-time team of alchemists at his castle and gathered together in his vast library astrologers, seers, fortune-tellers, as well as students of the occult like Edward Kelly and John Dee, to discuss the mysteries of metaphysics and the possibility of his being the first to break the secret code of life and of dominion over time and the elements, and thus becoming the first immortal king.

"I read a lot about John Dee for my study of the mirror in literature and in the magic arts through time," you said, "a book I am writing partly as a way of exorcising the fear of mirrors from which I have suffered since childhood. John Dee was also obsessed by mirrors. A mirror or *speculum* from his collection, a solid piece of glass the size of a tennis ball which he used in his experiments, is on show in the British Museum. The last time I saw it, my sight was much better than it is now, and I noticed that the *speculum* was giving off a mysterious light, like a pulsating halo. I commented on this to the person I was with, but he said: 'What light?'"

"You were the only one who could see it . . ."

"Yes, I was the only one. If I believed in such things, I would say that John Dee was trying to communicate with me across time, in a code known only to both ancient and new frequenters of the King of Bohemia's library, the real and the imaginary. I gave the matter no further thought."

"Because you don't believe in such things."

"I'm like a friend of mine who went to visit Chartres Cathedral and started levitating in front of one of the stained-glass windows, until he remembered that he wasn't a mystic and returned to earth."

"Imagine the marvels we would experience if we believed in the things in which we don't believe."

You were sitting with your head tilted slightly back. You remained silent for some time, a half-smile on your lips. Then you said:

"John Dee's *speculum* in the British Museum doubtless continues sending out its code 'for my eyes only', as top-secret documents in spy stories are always stamped. Except that my eyes aren't up to the task."

John Dee also had a theory that all the letters of the alphabet have magical stories, the history of their shape starting with the original one transmitted by God to Adam Kadmon, the First Man of the Kabbala, when He revealed to him His secret name. All the changes made to the alphabet since had been attempts to disguise that original shape, so that the secret name of God would never be written down by mistake. According to Dee, any combination of vowels and consonants was a combination of powerful mystical forces which only chance prevented from having grave conse-quences, for a text could, at any moment, and quite acci-dentally, destroy the world.

"Or, quite accidentally, reveal the secret vocabulary of the world," I said.

"Exactly! That is why the vowels in ancient Hebrew had

no written form. The name of God was an acronym of four consonants, the Tetragrammaton, so as to forestall the danger of some irresponsible person like you or me, Vogelstein, inserting the correct vowels and writing the complete name of God, in the belief that we were merely writing an epigram, and blowing up the Universe as a consequence."

"Without even leaving our chairs."

"I suspect that the American government's harsh treatment and segregation of the Cherokee Indians was not because they were deemed any more savage than other Indians, but because they were the only ones who had developed syllabic writing, because they were able to combine vowels and consonants and write things down in order to remember, thus giving their demons access to the written word."

"And they joined our tribe."

"Which is extremely dangerous. We writers should all be kept on reserves, under armed guard, and our literary production examined daily, the way ministers used to examine the faeces of the emperors of China so as to learn about their inner world."

"Hm," said the electric heater.

You went on, with a smile, knowing what my reaction would be:

"John Dee was the first man to speak of the Eternal Orangutan . . ."

"The what?!"

"That's right, another orangutan."

"What is the statistical probability of the same story containing two hypothetical orangutans?"

"About the same as the same Japanese man being knocked over twice at the same cocktail party."

"Probably."

"Dee's Eternal Orangutan, equipped with a sturdy quill, enough ink and an infinite surface to cover, would end up writing all the known books, as well as creating its own original works. Though these, as you might imagine, would be of dubious quality. It was because of the danger constituted by the Eternal Orangutan that, around 1585, Rudolf II managed to gather together in his library in Prague representatives of the three main gnostic philosophies: the Christian Apocrypha, born out of a supposed Second Book of Esdras not included in the Bible, the Judaic Kabbala, and a third strand, even more ancient and obscure, that had its origins in the magic lists of the library in Assurbanipal, which included the Necronomicon 'invented', according to Johnson, by Lovecraft."

"Lovecraft being a notorious modern example of the Eternal Orangutan in action, because he invented a truth that already existed."

"Precisely. We must not forget that, in 1585, Herr Gutenberg's terrible creation had already been in existence for more than a hundred years, books had become popularised and the Eternal Orangutan had at its hypothetical disposal not only all of eternity, but also movable type, with which to play at putting together vowels and consonants. This had increased the risk of the esoteric language being deciphered by mistake, or of someone stumbling upon the secret vocabulary of the Universe that the occultists were looking for and upon the power that this would bring. With the proliferation of writing, there was an increased risk of coincidence without which, of course, nothing in History can happen."

"I wrote a story once about a strike held by the gods. One by one, the gods that rule human existence go on strike, but this has absolutely no effect on anyone's life. The god of passion, the god of desires, the god of meanness and of munificence . . . None of these strikes has any effect on the destinies of men, apart from a few privations and misunderstandings. Only when the god of coincidences stops work does everyone's story change. In my story, entitled 'The God of Coincidences', Oedipus dies undramatically of old age, surrounded by his grandchildren, without ever learning his true story."

This was the second of the three stories I had sent you, Jorge, without ever receiving a reply. You gave no indication that you recognised it. You said:

"Without coincidence, the Eternal Orangutan could write for as long as it wanted and never come up with *Hamlet*. At most, it would rewrite one of the crude poems written by my distant cousin, Juan Carlos Borges, of whom you will not have heard. Indeed, we always suspected that his poems were, in fact, written by an ape."

I did not want to tell you that I had met your distant

cousin, not wishing to recount the circumstances of that meeting twenty-five years before. Just as I had avoided mentioning that Dee's Eternal Orangutan was the third hypothetical orangutan in our story, for you had mentioned another one in the letter of complaint you wrote about the tail appended to your story in *Mistério Magazine*. Did you or did you not know who I was, Jorge? On that magical night, was the game continuing or not?

You told how in the King of Bohemia's fantastical library they resorted to coincidence in their attempts to evoke the spiritual language that circulated in the spheres and in dreams and that sought expression and significance in words, in vowels and consonants. With eyes closed, they would remove a book from the shelves, open it at random, choose a line, and then immediately copy this down. The process was repeated until they had a reasonably coherent paragraph or one that was promisingly incoherent and open to interpretation. You remembered doing the same thing in the library of that other King of Bohemia, your father, and recalled the resulting marvellous stories, in which fairies lived alongside Roman tribunes, prostitutes quoted from Descartes and white whales suddenly surfaced in the pampas.

"They say that if John Dee concentrated hard, he could make books fly off the shelves and fall, open, on the floor of that library in Prague, and that everyone would then study the pages thus exposed and try to understand their message. For nothing happened by chance, everything was a message."

"That's what I think too. Everything *is* a message. Even the shape made by the hairs stuck in your bar of soap," I said.

You laughed and said:

"A form of communication with the beyond not available to blind bathers."

And then the old Indian woman dressed in black emerged like an apparition out of the surrounding darkness and passed on a message from "the mistress of the house". Borges needed to sleep. You spread wide your arms and said, smiling: "One must obey orders from above." As the maid was leaving, however, she bumped into a table and we heard the sound of a book falling to the floor. You immediately ordered her to leave the book where it was and asked me to fetch it. It was a selection of Poe's stories that you had removed from the shelf in order to refresh your memory when you heard the surprising news that the conference of the Israfel Society would be taking place in Buenos Aires, and that your participation, however minimal, would be required. You asked:

"Did the book fall open?"

"It did," I replied.

"At which story?"

"'The Gold-Bug'."

"Of course."

Then you said that the death of the unfortunate Rotkopf had at least given us this opportunity to meet and talk and reach conclusions.

"But we haven't reached any conclusions!" I protested.

"All the better," you said. "It's an excuse to talk further."

And in the midst of the darkness that separated our enchanted circle from the door of your library, I heard you say in your velvety voice:

"We haven't even discussed the blind jack of spades yet!"

I WAS WOKEN THE NEXT MORNING BY A PHONE CALL from my cousin Pipo. The story of the murder had appeared in all the newspapers, my name had been mentioned and, according to Pipo, my Aunt Sofia was very worried. He had mobilised his staff and they, miraculously, had tracked me down. I could count on him for any help I might need. If it came to it, he could even get me a lawyer, the best in Buenos Aires. I thanked him and said that I didn't need anything, but would keep him informed. I asked after Aunt Sofia, and Pipo, unaware that he was contradicting himself, said she was fine, but that she wasn't really aware of what was going on around her and talked nothing but gibberish in what appeared to be German. Pipo's voice had grown shriller with the years. I ordered breakfast in my room and stayed in bed, thinking with pleasure, Jorge, of our conversation the previous night, until I had to get up to remove the chain and open the door to the waiter bearing my breakfast. That night I imagine all the hotel guests slept with their doors securely locked.

As you will remember, Jorge, it was a day of news. The biggest news was that Cuervo and his team had, that morning, discovered not one, but three knives in the hotel.

The hotel had two narrow ventilation shafts. The bathroom windows of rooms with numbers ending in 1 and 2 gave onto one of these, and rooms with numbers ending in 4 and 5 onto the other. The bathrooms in rooms with numbers ending in 3, like room 703, in which Rotkopf had been knifed to death, had no window. Two knives had been found at the bottom of the shaft that served rooms 701 and 702, the other at the bottom of the shaft that served room 704. None of the knives bore any traces of blood, but all three – an excited Cuervo informed me, when we met in the hotel foyer at around midday – were being examined in the laboratory.

The previous night, while you and I were discussing hypothetical gatherings of gnostics in sixteenth-century Prague, Cuervo had been doing his job. He had spoken to the occupant of room 701, who was none other than the Japanese gentleman who had been knocked over twice at the cocktail party; he was a professor of English and American literature from Kyoto called Ikisara, who attended all the Israfel

Society conferences and was to appear at this conference at a round table on Poe's female characters. He told the police that he had heard my noisy arrival at the hotel with Rotkopf, had seen me going into the German's room, only to leave again after twenty minutes, visibly drunk. Later, at half past eleven, he had been woken by the sound of someone pounding violently on Rotkopf's door and shouting "Open up! It's Johnson!" The pounding had been repeated several times, but by the time he got to the door to complain about the noise, there was no-one to be seen, and he didn't know if Johnson had gone into Rotkopf's room or back into his own. Half an hour later, the Japanese professor was again woken by someone pounding on Rotkopf's door and a voice yelling "Open up! It's Urquiza!" Again, by the time he got to the door, he found the corridor empty. He could not tell whether Rotkopf had opened the door to Urquiza or if Urquiza had given up and returned to his room. Finally, at dawn, Professor Ikisara had been woken by my insistent pounding on the German's door and had half-opened the door to his own room. Seeing my unusually agitated state, he had continued to watch everything that happened in the corridor from then on. He had seen me go tearing off only to return accompanied by the night porter. He had seen us break down the door. He had seen the night porter, eyes wide with fear, rush off to the lift, then, six or seven minutes later, had watched as various people invaded the corridor, emerging from the elevator and from the stairs. And he had observed with horror that everyone who emerged from room 703 had blood on their shoes.

"Three knives!"

"Three. Of different sizes. All three had clearly been thrown down the shafts recently. The criminal investigation department will tell us which of the three was used in the murder."

"Perhaps all three were used."

"Oh, please . . ." said Cuervo, dramatically pressing his fingertips to his temples, in anticipation of a headache. "*Anything* but rituals."

"Borges will like the fact that there were three knives," I said.

"Yes, Borges will," sighed Cuervo, as if that were a further reason for his probable migraine.

After lunching together, we arranged to go back to your library to bring you the latest news.

During lunch, Cuervo told me that, as foreseen, he had run into problems when interviewing Oliver Johnson, who had agreed to answer questions, but only in the presence of a representative from the United States consulate. Johnson had denied knocking on Rotkopf's door at half past eleven. He regretted Dr Rotkopf's death, but could not say he was exactly surprised. Rotkopf was a provoking, exasperating man, and if he had had the chance, he himself . . . Johnson had stopped there, realising that, if he *had* knocked on Rotkopf's door and Rotkopf *had* opened it, then he would have had just such a chance, as well as a reason for denying he had knocked on the door.

Johnson had agreed to remain in Buenos Aires for a few more days until everything was cleared up, but he would not be staying at the hotel. The consulate would provide alternative lodging for him.

"And Urquiza?" I asked.

"He too denies knocking on Rotkopf's door at some time around midnight. He repeated his assertion that he heard nothing of what occurred in room 703."

"Assuming one of the two is lying and is, in fact, the murderer, either the half-past-eleven murderer or the midnight murderer, how is it that Rotkopf telephoned me at three in the morning?"

"He could have been knifed any time after you left him in his room. He could have taken hours to die. He could have taken hours to drag himself over to the phone."

"And then drag himself over to the mirror."

"Ah, yes, to leave the murderer's initial . . ."

Cuervo obviously did not share our enthusiasm for the dead man's cryptographic efforts, Jorge.

I too had news. Well, two bits of news, but only one I could talk about. When I arrived at the hotel the previous night, I met Angela in reception. The suspension of the conference was proving very demanding for the conference stewards, who had to deal with cancelled reservations and changed flights, as well as provide succour to the stunned participants. Angela was exhausted and suggested we go up to my room for a drink. She began taking off her clothes even before room service had arrived, and we left the whiskies untouched on the bedside table. Confronted by her nakedness and her affectionate ardour, I qualified as another stunned participant. She had a mole between her two breasts and another exactly halfway between that and her navel, forming, with her nipples and the mole on her forehead, a kind of pointillist cross, in disconcerting symmetry; but what would have pleased Aunt Raquel most was the fact that she was Jewish. A Jewish angel called Angela. When Pipo's phone call woke me, she had already gone. The news I could talk about, only omitting the fact that the thought had occurred to me as I was lying with my head between those angelic breasts, was that Rotkopf's V-shaped body had not been lying with its bottom against the mirror, as I had said. I was wrong. As I lay on the cross of Angela's body, after love and at peace, I was able to remember more clearly. Only the feet of Rotkopf's V-shaped body had been resting against the mirror and its bottom had been facing the bedroom door. When I had gone in through the door, I had seen not an X, but a W!

I decided not to contribute to Cuervo's incipient headache with this information. I would save it for you, Borges. I asked:

"So, is it X for Xavier or O for Oliver?"

"It could be either. If one of the two denied having

knocked on Rotkopf's door, then he would be the natural suspect, but they both deny it. And if both of them knocked on Rotkopf's door, to which of them did Rotkopf open up? Johnson knocked first, according to the Japanese gentleman, so he is the main suspect. But either of them could have killed Rotkopf, gone back to his own room and thrown the knife out of the bathroom window. Both windows open onto ventilation shafts."

"But in one of the shafts there were two knives."

"I know," said Cuervo, with the look of someone who would have preferred not to be reminded of this. "The ventilation shaft that serves the bathroom in room 702, Oliver's room, and that of room 701 . . ."

"The Japanese gentleman's room."

"Yes, Dr Ikisara's room . . ."

Cuervo sighed again.

"Borges and I would prefer the murderer to be Oliver Johnson," I said.

"Why's that?"

"Because the literary possibilities are far more promising. The story could then begin in ancient Egypt."

Cuervo did not even smile. He was wondering what would be worse, having to accuse an American, an illustrious fellow Argentinian who would inevitably use his social position to avoid being tried, or an irritable Japanese professor whose only apparent motive for murder was that the murder victim had twice knocked him over at a cocktail party. The laboratory tests would resolve part of the mystery, but whoever the murderer was, there was still the matter of how he had managed to leave a locked room without unlocking the door.

On the way to your house, Borges, I told Cuervo about our conversation of the previous night. He told me how the police had searched all five rooms on the seventh floor, and made a very careful search of the dead man's room and of room 705, occupied by a salesman from Córdoba who said he had no idea what was going on, had never even heard of Edgar Allan Poe, or, to be honest, of any other pop stars. Nothing had been found in Rotkopf's room, apart from his clothes, which included an unusually large number of woollen socks. There was no lecture, no notes, no sheets of paper of any kind with writing on them. Unless all his papers had been stolen, Rotkopf had apparently been planning to begin the conference with an entirely extempore speech. Urquiza had refused to open his suitcases. Johnson had opened his only under protest and shown them the text of his talk about Lovecraft, Poe and the *Necronomicon*, with its as yet unpublished revelations, as well as other papers he had with him. No-one appeared to have stolen anything from Rotkopf's room. Amongst Professor Ikisara's papers was a letter from the organisers of the conference, in reply to what had clearly been a discourteous enquiry from the Japanese, explaining why the Israfel Society had, exceptionally, decided to hold the conference in Buenos Aires. Their answer had not convinced Professor Ikisara.

"Three knives!"

You were radiant, Borges. When we arrived, you told us that you hadn't felt so well in ages. You felt rejuvenated and in the mood to write.

"Who knows, Vogelstein, I might turn out to be John Dee's Eternal Orangutan. I will live for ever and write everything that was ever written in the world. After all, I've already written a good part of it."

Cuervo was too absorbed in his own doubts to ask who this new orangutan was. You went on:

"And one day, I will, quite by chance, put together the fatal vowels and consonants, and the world will disappear. Since, as far as I'm concerned, the world has already disappeared, I won't notice any difference. I will continue dictating my books for ever, inside this library, wondering only why they are taking so long to bring me my tea. Or will the eternity of the hypothetical Orangutan end when he writes the secret name of God? What do you think, Vogelstein?"

"I don't know," I said. "If eternity is infinite, not even the end of everything will destroy it. I see the Orangutan surviving alone, after everything and everyone has gone, including God. He will be the last author."

"They'll have no option but to give him the Nobel Prize, don't you think, Vogelstein?"

"Absolutely."

It was then that Cuervo, impatient with our conversation, interrupted it with a report on the investigations so far and the news of the three knives. And you were amazed:

"Three knives!"

You mentioned that Palermo, the part of Buenos Aires where you were brought up, had been a violent place full of bohemians and bandits. There they had two names for the knife, "the blade" and "the slicer". The two names described the same object, but "the blade" was the thing itself, and "the slicer" described its function. "The blade" could fit in the hand even of a sickly child shut up in his father's library, "the blade" could be any of the superannuated daggers and swords belonging to his warrior grandfather or great-grandfather and displayed on the walls of his house, but "the slicer", the knife in the hand slicing back and forth, in and out, existed only in his imagination, in a fascinating world of rapid settlings of accounts and duels over honour, an insult or a woman, in dark streets where you never went, where no writer went, except in the literature he wrote.

"I've always felt that in order to be a great writer, one should have experience of life at sea, which is why Conrad and Melville and, in a way, Stevenson, who ended his days in the South Seas, were better than all of us, Vogelstein. At sea, a writer flees from the minor demons and faces only the definitive ones. A character in Conrad says that he has

84

a horror of ports because, in port, ships rot and men go to the devil. He meant the devils of domesticity and incoherence, the small devils of terra firma. But I think that having experience of 'the slicer' would give a writer the same sensation as going to sea, of spectacularly breaking the bounds of his own passivity and of his remoteness from the fundamental matters of the world."

"You mean that if a writer were to stab someone three times, he could allege that he was merely doing so in order to improve his style."

"Something like that. Soaking up experience and atmosphere."

"It's said that the artist Turner used to have himself lashed to the ship's mast during storms at sea so that he could make sure he was getting the colours and details of his painted vortices right."

"And it worked. But neither you nor I will ever experience 'the slicer', Vogelstein. We are condemned to 'the blade', to the knife purely as theory. Even if we used 'the slicer' against someone, we would still be ourselves, watching, analysing the scene, and, therefore, inevitably, holding 'the blade' in our hand. I don't think I could kill anyone, apart from my own characters. And I don't think I would feel comfortable at sea either. There aren't any libraries at sea. The sea replaces the library."

"Jules Verne's Captain Nemo had the sea and a library."

"Yes, but not, as far as we know, any literary talent."

"So what do you think?" asked Cuervo.

"About what?" you said.

"About the three knives. About the knocking on Rotkopf's door. About the locked room. Where does it all leave us?"

Cuervo did not appear to be enjoying his lunch. You squeezed your lower lip between thumb and forefinger to show that you were thinking, or perhaps to conceal from Cuervo your smile of pleasure. We really had restored your health and your good humour with our sheet of blood and our enigmas, Jorge.

"Well . . . We have Rotkopf staying on the same floor as his two adversaries, or three adversaries, if we count the Japanese gentleman who got knocked over twice. There were three stab wounds in the body, and now three knives have been found in two ventilation shafts . . . If nature teaches us anything, gentlemen, it is to distrust too much symmetry. Two threads of hair forming the profile of Buddha or of W.C. Fields on a bar of soap is chance, two threads of hair forming a perfectly centred cross is a message. Excessive symmetry is either unnatural and conceals some human thought behind it, or else supernatural and conceals some mystery."

You were in good form, Jorge, perched on the edge of your armchair.

"Where does that leave us, you ask. We have a lying oriental and two lying occidentals. If the oriental was telling the truth, then one of the two lying occidentals is guilty. But why would both occidentals deny having knocked on the victim's door? One – the guilty party – so as not to incriminate himself, of course, but the other one?"

"So as not to incriminate himself either, even though he's innocent," I suggested.

"But if Urquiza knew that Johnson had knocked on Rotkopf's door before he did, he would have no need to lie. He could easily say that, yes, he had knocked on the door and Rotkopf hadn't answered for the obvious reason that he had already been stabbed to death – by Johnson."

"And what if the Japanese gentleman was lying?" asked Cuervo.

I jumped in with an answer:

"Then he is the guilty party. He alone knocked on Rotkopf's door, killed him and then threw the knife through the bathroom window. And he invented the other two men knocking at the door in order to incriminate them."

"And what about the other two knives?" Cuervo enquired.

"No idea," I replied, very unscientifically.

You were shaking your head.

"No, the Japanese gentleman didn't lie and neither did Urquiza. The only liar in this story is Oliver Johnson."

"But the Japanese professor said that he heard Urquiza knocking on Rotkopf's door, and Urquiza denies it!"

"Because Urquiza wasn't knocking on Rotkopf's door. According to your account, Cuervo, the Japanese professor only heard Urquiza knocking on someone's door at midnight and shouting 'Open up, it's Urquiza.' How can we be sure that it was Rotkopf's door? It could have been Johnson's door."

"But he wouldn't have been able to open the door because, at that moment, he was in Rotkopf's room stabbing him three times with 'the slicer'!" I cried.

"Or else unsuccessfully trying to persuade Rotkopf not to discredit him the following day," you went on. "Rotkopf doubtless replied with his irritating little jingle: 'Israfel, Israfel, does it ring a bell?', and Johnson would have been unable to restrain himself. Who would?"

There was a pained expression on Cuervo's face.

"And what would Urquiza have wanted with Johnson?" he asked.

"Perhaps to dissuade him from presenting his talk on the *Necronomicon* and then, if Johnson refused, he would have killed him."

I completed your thesis, Jorge, in literary style.

"Johnson is in Rotkopf's room when he telephones me at three o'clock in the morning. They have been arguing since half past eleven. Johnson searches the room, looking for Rotkopf's lecture, while Rotkopf is dying on his sheet of blood. Johnson notices, too late, that Rotkopf is still alive and has managed to reach the phone and dial someone's number. He rushes out, perhaps after stabbing Rotkopf for a third time, and goes to his room, closing the door only seconds before I get out of the elevator. He cleans the murder weapon and throws it out of the bathroom window."

"Before that," you continued, "Urquiza had given up knocking on Johnson's door and also returned to his own room. The following day, when he finds out about Rotkopf's murder, he decides, just in case, to throw his knife out of the bathroom window."

"All right," said Cuervo, clutching his head. "We've explained two of the knives. What about the third?"

Jorge and I were unanimous in our silence.

"And how did Johnson manage to leave the room without unlocking the door?" insisted Cuervo.

We continued in silence. Until you, trying, out of respect for Cuervo's distress, not to sound ironic, said:

"Well, there are still a few details to be worked out . . ."

I asked what you meant about too much symmetry. You revealed that you also had some news. Taking advantage of your previous night's insomnia, you had been rummaging around in the depths of your memory for everything you knew about the *Necronomicon*, and about your researches into John Dee. You had remembered that the power of the magical beings, of the dead names, was shared out amongst the quadrants of the Earth, and that the most powerful beings were Azathoth and Yog-Sothoth, from the Southern quadrant, the king and the prince of chaos, the only ones who could call up Hastur, he who walked in the wind, the destroyer. You had a vague idea that something linked Hastur to the case in hand and finally, as the night was ending, you remembered what it was: in the contents page of the translation of the Necronomicon that Lovecraft attributed to John Dee, the chapter on Hastur was number ten. The X that Rotkopf had made in the mirror. The number 10 card that accompanied the prince and the king of the pack. And surely we remembered that sudden wind on the night of the crime.

If your intention had been to irritate Cuervo still further, you succeeded. He was standing up.

"Do you mean to say that the murderer isn't Johnson now, but Hastur, a malign spirit?"

"At least that solves the problem of the locked room. After all, spirits can walk through walls," I said provocatively.

"Or perhaps Johnson was the embodiment of Hastur, since he had presumably deciphered all the spells in the Necronomicon," you added.

"Can we be serious for a moment?" Cuervo pleaded.

"Do you not find it a serious matter that, for the first time in its history, the Israfel Society decided to hold its conference in the South, and that Rotkopf, Urquiza and Johnson all ended up on the same floor in the same hotel? Perhaps they were there under the jurisdiction of Azathoth and Yog-Sothoth, the king and prince of chaos, in order to kill each other. Not to mention the Japanese professor, who was suspicious of the intentions of the board of the Israfel Society, about which, by the way, almost nothing is known."

"There's just one thing," I said, embarrassed.

"What's that?"

"It wasn't an X."

"What wasn't an X?"

"The shape made by Rotkopf's body in the mirror. It was a W."

Cuervo would accept no excuses. All that time wasted because I had misremembered! But I noticed that you were squeezing your lower lip again and that your thoughts had already set off along another path. You said:

"A W . . . Interesting. The symbol of the double, of duality, of twins, of the doppelgänger. Poe has a story entitled 'William Wilson', about a man destroyed by his own double, by his image in the mirror, which is his moral self. I myself have always been rather afraid of mirrors . . ."

"I know."

"What was Rotkopf trying to tell us with that W? It isn't the name of any of the possible suspects. Unless . . . The Japanese gentleman's first name isn't Watanabe, is it?"

"No," said Cuervo. "It's Miro."

"And what if Rotkopf was trying to tell us that he had been attacked by his own reflection in the mirror?" you asked. "By his moral self. Judging by what is known of

Rotkopf's character, his opposite must be an example to us all, a monster of rectitude. That's it, the murderer was the German's conscience, which, unable to contain its disgust at what it was forced to reflect, leaped out of the mirror. In the Poe story, the moral self puts up with everything until he can stand it no longer, until William Wilson commits an unforgivable outrage. What could have provoked Rotkopf's double finally to kill him?"

"Now that I think about it, I didn't see Rotkopf's walking stick next to his body. His reflection must have taken it with him, when he fled through the locked window of the room."

"A technical question. If Rotkopf's reflection did kill him and flee, Rotkopf's body could not be reflected in the mirror. It would just be a V lying against an empty mirror."

"And where did the reflection in the mirror manage to get hold of the reflection of a knife to use?"

Cuervo gave up. He had more important things to do than to stay there listening to such madness. He needed to continue his investigation of the crime, using science not fantasies, and since we were clearly both raving, he obviously couldn't count on us for our help any more. Before leaving, he announced that he was going to oblige the board of the Israfel Society to appear and show themselves. Amongst other things, he needed their help on what to do with Rotkopf's body, for the man had no known family, either in Mexico or in Germany.

After Cuervo left, we sat on in silence, listening to the hum of the heater. We needed an audience. After a few minutes, you said:

"Apparently there's a double of myself loose in Buenos Aires. It's one of the myths people have invented about me. The last time I could see myself clearly in the mirror, my image had fled, in order to save itself from my decline. Friends tell me that they sometimes see my double in the street, and that he has very acute eyesight, so acute that he can see the craters on the Moon without the aid of a telescope, but that he lacks imagination. It must be some kind of standard compensation awarded only to authors, imagination instead of sight. Think of Joyce."

"And Homer."

"And Akhenaten."

"Was Akhenaten blind?"

"He ended up blind. They say he mutilated himself after some tale of incest and guilt, like Oedipus. It seems the Egyptians were in the habit of being Greeks before their time, especially the pharaohs."

"But Akhenaten wasn't a writer."

"He was the one who thought up monotheism and invented God. He might not have been a writer, but he had a gift for creating good characters. Now my double, they say, is not involved in any literary activity whatsoever, in fact, he has even been seen attacking bookshops and vandalising libraries. He hates books, which he calls the enemies of life."

Again, so as not to have to describe the circumstances of the encounter, I did not tell you that I had also met your opposite, Borges Luis Jorge. Instead, I told the third story I had sent you, and which, like the first two, you had ignored. A story based, in fact, on my visit to Buenos Aires to find you. A man travels to a city in the South in search of a master writer and finds a magical city, consisting solely of places that the writer has described – the house in which he was born, the houses where he had lived, the school he studied at, the bars and bookshops he frequented, etc. The rest of the city does not exist, it consists only of lacunae in between the places that the visitor recognises from the fiction and the memoirs of the writer. There are only two dogs and one tram in the city: the dogs that the writer remembered from his childhood and the only tram described in his work. But there is no-one on the streets of the city. When he does finally meet someone – a beggar-poet whom the visitor identifies as the character from a parable written by the writer – the character says to him, in verse, that the whole population of the city is in the only church, the church in which the writer was baptised. And there too are all the writer's characters, as well as his father and mother, his grandparents and great-grandparents, and the schoolfellows, lovers and friends mentioned in his books, all standing vigil over the writer's corpse. And while they wait, they gradually disappear one by one, until only three or four are left around the coffin, in the midst of nothing, for the church itself and the city have also disappeared. Among those remaining is a literary critic — venomously portrayed by the master writer as a thinly disguised character — who looks around him and remarks to the visitor: "I always said not much of his work would survive . . .", and then he disappears too.

Again, you gave no sign of recognising the story. When I finished, you sat, squeezing your lower lip, and thinking. Then you said:

"The W is no use to us. The W is no use to us at all, my dear Vogelstein."

I got up to go, but you asked me to stay. Perhaps we would be lucky and some book would fly off the shelves and fall open at our feet, to reveal the pages that would resolve everything. And for the remainder of that evening, we talked about English authors of the nineteenth century and which of them we could possibly imagine committing a murder untainted by the curse of self-consciousness, thus transforming "the blade" into "the slicer". We also talked about symmetry in your own work, do you remember? About how you published your first detective story, "The Garden of Forking Paths", exactly one hundred years after Poe had published his first story, and other apparent coincidences. And we drank tea.

M

THE THIRD DAY. THIS TIME THE PHONE CALL THAT WAKES me is from Cuervo. He has the results from the laboratory. Science has been doing its work. Microscopic traces of blood on one of the knives show that this was the only one used in the crime. It is one of the two found in the ventilation shaft leading away from the bathroom windows of 701 and 702. The blood on the knife belongs to Rotkopf, of that there is no doubt. The murderer is either Johnson or the Japanese professor. Urquiza is innocent. There are no fingerprints on any of the knives. They will now investigate where the three knives came from. I ask if he has found out anything more about the Israfel Society. Cuervo says that he is struggling to persuade Urquiza, the society's representative in Argentina, to help him. Urquiza has announced that he will be going back to Mendoza as soon as Rotkopf's body has been despatched somewhere, and that he intends to forget all about the case, including the ignominy of being counted amongst the suspects. Cuervo may have to mobilise the Minister of Justice in order to keep Urquiza in Buenos Aires and force him to cooperate.

And what about you, Cuervo asks me. Can you stay on longer in Buenos Aires to help with the investigations? I hesitate. The previous night, Angela came to my room again. After we had made love, she advised me to return home. She would take care of my ticket, she would take care of everything. There was no need for me to stay in Buenos Aires. I had done my bit. I should distance myself from the whole bloody episode and try to forget everything that had happened. I agree with her, but then I think of you, Jorge. I think about our evenings together. When will I have another opportunity like this to talk to you? My hotel room is reserved for another four days. Nothing requires my return to Porto Alegre and to Bonfim for another week yet. Not even a cat. I tell Cuervo that I need to think about it. I want to help, but I cannot do more than I have already done. And my memory, after all, is neither a reliable nor a very precise informant, as Cuervo has already discovered. I do not tell him that the previous night, while I lay in Angela's arms, on the pointillist cross of her body, I went over again in my mind what I had seen when I entered Rotkopf's room after the murder and realised that I had made yet another mistake. I had not seen a V with one end touching the mirror and the vertex facing the door, forming a W in the mirror. I had seen the V with one end touching the mirror and the open part facing the door, thus forming an M in the mirror.

When I get up to unlock the door for the waiter bringing my breakfast, I notice that Angela took my ticket with her when she left this morning without waking me.

I lunched alone near the hotel. Afterwards, I started walking along Calle Suipacha trying to decide what to do. To return at once to Porto Alegre or not to return? A black car drew up alongside the curb. It was Cuervo, summoning me to go with him to your house, Jorge. He had some news.

You did not seem to be in such good form on that third day, Jorge. The Indian servant warned us at the door, "el señor Borges is tired". We mustn't stay long. Cuervo told us that, by threatening to make an official request to the Ministry of Justice, he had finally managed to get Urquiza to talk to him about the Israfel Society. All we knew was that the society had been in existence since 1937, that it promoted the study of Edgar Allan Poe's work, organised the conferences and published various bulletins, including the monthly journal, The Gold-Bug. Cuervo had taken part in two conferences, both of them in Baltimore. According to Urquiza, the society's headquarters was in Boston, where Poe had been born, and the journal was based in Baltimore, where Poe had died. The society had been founded by a Czech called Partas, who had emigrated to the United States in the early 1930s, made his fortune, and was still the main financial backer and director of its activities, although he never attended any events or ceremonies. Urquiza went to all the conferences and was a kind of honorary representative of the society in Argentina. That very morning he had received a phone call from Boston, instructing him to send Rotkopf's body to Cuernavaca as soon as it was released by the Argentinian authorities, so that it could be buried in a place chosen by the German – far, I thought, from any hint of shade.

"Did Urquiza say why the conference was being held in Buenos Aires this year?" you asked.

"He said it was at his, Urquiza's, request, which I find hard to believe."

"Why?"

"Because in their letter to the Japanese professor, the board of the Israfel Society gave a completely different reason," said Cuervo. "And Urquiza wasn't involved in the organisation of the conference. He travelled in from Mendoza on the opening day."

"Angela told me that the stewards for the conference were hired by an American team who arrived in Buenos Aires from Baltimore two weeks before, to organise everything," I said.

"And who have since left," reported Cuervo. "None of the organisers is here. At least I haven't met any. The bills were paid, everything was sorted out, but the Israfel Society has vanished. The stewards were left in charge of the early return of conference participants and told to submit any bills later, but that's as much as they know."

"Who booked Urquiza, Johnson and Rotkopf into rooms on the same floor in the same hotel?" you asked.

"The distribution of the rooms was decided beforehand."

"Apart from a few last-minute changes," I put in. "As in my case."

"In your case?"

"I was booked into another hotel. Angela moved me to the one in Calle Suipacha because it was more central."

"So you got involved in this whole story by chance . . ."

Or by luck, I thought. If I hadn't got involved that way, I wouldn't have met you, and I probably wouldn't have slept with Angela, the two most memorable events of my entire life until now, since I have no memory of the journey by ship from Germany to Brazil.

Cuervo and I sat looking at you, as if we had put the right coins in the machine and were now awaiting our bar of chocolate. You were sitting with your head bowed. When you spoke, your voice was softer and weaker than it usually was.

"Partas from Czechoslovakia. Partas from Prague. Partas from former Bohemia. Partas, Partas, Partas . . . Do you know what I think?"

We didn't, but we were dying to know.

"I think that it all went wrong. It was supposed to work as smoothly as Swiss clockwork, or as Czech clockwork in this case, but you cannot with impunity bring a delicate mechanism from the north and expect it to work in the south. Here the moon waxes and wanes the other way round, something that can even disorient Americans. If this were my story . . ."

And you told us what the story would be like if you had written it. Urquiza was to kill Johnson. Urquiza was to invoke the powerful beings from the South, Azathoth and Yog-Sothoth, and to be the embodiment of Hastur, the destroyer, he who walks in the wind, so as to prevent Johnson from revealing even more than he already had, quite innocently, revealed of the language of the Necronomicon and of the secret code concealed in Poe's literature. Everything had been set up with that end in mind. The conference was moved to Buenos Aires in order to bring Johnson to the South, where Urquiza would invoke the powers of Azathoth and Yog-Sothoth as well as Hastur's lethal skill with "the slicer" to eliminate him without leaving any traces . . . But Partas, or whoever had laid the trap for Johnson, had failed to take into account intellectual vanity, a force more destructive than any other, known or unknown, the most terrible force in the Universe — Pride, our overwhelming love of ourselves. Weary of the German's insults, horrified at the prospect of being ridiculed in public, Johnson knocks on Rotkopf's door and kills him.

"So Rotkopf also entered the story by chance," I said.

"And his murder disassembled the trap and ruined all their plans. Johnson was killing Rotkopf when he should have been in his room, awaiting Urquiza's knife. And Urquiza knocked and knocked on his door and then gave up. With the discovery of Rotkopf's body, of course, every-thing fell apart. Urquiza threw away his knife and is now about to go back to Mendoza; the organisers of the confer-ence have scattered; and Johnson, protected by the American embassy, will deny that the bloodstained knife is his, saying that there is absolutely no proof that he killed Rotkopf, and will fly home without a stain on his character. If his plane falls out of the skies before he crosses the Equator, then we will know that, as well as being powerful, Azathoth and Yog-Sothoth, the beings of the South, are also vengeful."

For some time now, Cuervo had been squirming in his armchair.

"Really, Jorge!" he said at last. "Gozatoth, Soga-Tog . . . You don't believe in all that!"

"Don't confuse the author with the characters," you replied. "I don't believe in anything. The important thing is that they do."

"Are you saying that the Israfel Society is a murderous organisation, ruled by malign spirits?"

"The Israfel Society has probably never murdered anyone, indeed, they failed on this first attempt. I suspect that it is one of many organisations with representatives all around the world who are constantly on the alert for the accidental discovery of gnostic codes by people who do not understand them, or for the appearance of new secret messages in the work of authors who often do not know exactly what they are transmitting when they write about things they have never themselves experienced. All these organisations form part of a kind of alarm system created, I believe, exactly 400 years ago, at a gathering of gnostics in Prague, in the library of the King of Bohemia, probably summoned by a man called John Dee, and which could be dubbed 'Operation Eternal Orangutan'."

"Oh, Jorge, really!"

"Let us not forget that the Israfel Society was created in the year of the death of Lovecraft. Its mission must be to keep a check on the followers and students of Poe and ensure that no-one else follows Lovecraft's example and stumbles upon another explosive revelation like that of the *Necronomicon*. There is always the risk that some other Johnson will interpret Poe, not wisely, but too well and have to be eliminated. What better way of keeping an eye on those who study Poe and compete amongst themselves for new ways of interpreting him than by organising conferences where they can discuss their theories, and by providing a forum where they can be published?"

"Let us not forget," said Cuervo, who had risen indignantly to his feet now, "that Xavier Urquiza is a practising, conservative Catholic who would never ally himself with a Gogagot or a Gogathot or any other occult demon, even one native to Patagonia."

Your voice had grown still weaker, Jorge. Cuervo had to bend down, like a heron hunting for a fish, to hear you.

"Taking part in this, so to speak, summit in King Rudolf II's library in 1585 were the adherents of an occultist strand of Christianity, the 'Apocrypha', whose key text was the Second Book of Esdras, expurgated from the Bible, which, in turn, was one of the basic texts in the Kabbala. Pico della Mirandola, who wanted to bring the Renaissance Church and the Kabbala closer together in order to combat secularism, went so far as to allege that the text proved that, in its most primitive form, Judaism was Trinitarian and foresaw the advent of Christ. As far as one knows, the Kabbala was withdrawn from the black conference arranged by Rudolf II, but John Dee managed to maintain the alliance between the philokabbalist Church of the 'Apocrypha' and the Necronomicon strand, whose origins probably lie in Egyptian hermeticism, pre-dating even Akhenaten. The Israfel Society is Christian. Its conferences, which are always held either in Stockholm, Baltimore or Prague — North, West and East — equate to a sign of the cross, to the sacred triangle. Urquiza may be an even more conservative Christian than people think and belong to the ancient occultist tradition of the Church, which has never emerged from the shadows, and which is willing to collaborate with any group that formed part of the black pact in Prague, in order to protect its codes and its secret powers."

Cuervo was now gazing up at the ceiling, as if asking for help.

"All right. Johnson killed Rotkopf and threw away the knife. Urquiza abandoned his attempt to kill Johnson and threw away his knife. What about the third knife?"

"It belonged to the Japanese professor, who probably also intended killing Rotkopf and had bought a knife on his way to the hotel. He got rid of it when he realised that someone else had done his work for him."

"And how did Johnson get out of the locked room after killing Rotkopf?"

You merely opened your arms wide, as if to allow yourself to be frisked. Cuervo went on:

"And what about the messages left by Rotkopf? And the cards? And the body against the mirror forming a W?"

"An M," I said.

You and Cuervo in unison:

"What?"

Me:

"I've been thinking about it. Two good nights' sleep have helped my memory. It wasn't a W. It was an M."

Cuervo fell back into his armchair without saying a word. You were smiling. You said:

"An M . . ."

108

"I'm almost certain."

"When are you going to be completely certain, Vogelstein?" cried Cuervo angrily.

But you shushed him. You had already set off along another path. You were thinking.

"M for Miro," I suggested. "The Japanese professor was the murderer . . ."

The suggestion found no takers. Cuervo had clearly lost all faith in my memory. You were once again squeezing your lower lip. To conclude with the Japanese professor as the culprit would be an unacceptable anticlimax.

"We have to combine the two clues," you said at last. "One makes no sense without the other. What do the cards show?"

"The cards don't show anything," said Cuervo.

"Exactly. And what do the cards not show?"

"What do you mean, not show?"

"What is missing in the sequence 10 of clubs, jack of spades and king of hearts?"

"The queen of diamonds," I said.

"Exactly. The queen."

"Do you mean the M stands for Mother?!" asked Cuervo.

"Or Mater. Or Mary. Don't forget, she is the queen of diamonds."

You went on:

"At the conference in Prague, the Christians of the 'Apocrypha' and the Jews of the Kabbala were unable to agree because the Jews would not accept the Christian interpretation of the Second Book of Esdras, according to which primitive Judaism acknowledged Jesus and the Trinity, thus allowing an approximation between Church and Kabbala. In the dispute, both sides had accused each other of treachery. The Christians accused the Jews of having betrayed Jesus, and the Jews accused the Christians of having betrayed their own mother, that is, Judaism, out of which they had been born. This was a dispute that had already been going on for 1,500 years and which continues today, in secret, between the Kabbala and Christian gnosis."

"Christianity belongs to the history of Judaic superstitions," I said, quoting you, more or less. Or one of your characters.

But you weren't listening.

"Have we got a new murderer, then?" asked Cuervo. "Rotkopf's mother perhaps, as the embodiment of Hastur?"

You ignored Cuervo too. You sat for a long time in silence, while Cuervo, without getting up from his chair, performed an impatient tap dance on the parquet. Then to me you addressed what seemed to be a chance remark, apropos of nothing:

"My mother must have had Jewish blood. Her surname was Acevedo. Perhaps a Portuguese Jew."

"Yes, I know."

Another long silence, broken only by the sound of Cuervo's static tap dancing. Then:

"Stockholm, Baltimore, Prague. Father, Son and Holy Ghost. North, West, East. The sign of the cross, the sacred triangle. What is missing from the triangle? Some might say the Mother, the great omission from the Trinity. Others say the Devil. At any rate, what's missing is the South."

"Rotkopf was trying to tell us something about the reason why the conference was being held in the South," I ventured.

"He would have been trusting too much to our ability to solve cryptograms if he was expecting us to make an instantaneous link between the M of mother and what's missing from the triangle. But the cards complete the message. Queen. Woman. Mother. Or the Devil. The prophet Esdras considered woman and the Devil to be the same thing. According to his banned book, the monsters that inhabit the Earth were children conceived during a woman's menstruation. They were the fruit of the female curse."

"So now we have a southerly point and the triangle becomes a lozenge."

"All right," said Cuervo. "Rotkopf makes a sign in the mirror meaning woman, and this is confirmed by the missing card. The woman and/or the Devil somewhere in the South. But what exactly does it mean?"

"Vogelstein," you said, "what did Rotkopf tell you about the trick he played on Johnson, inventing a hidden meaning for the poem 'Israfel'?"

"He said that there are two versions of the poem, the second shorter than the first, with a few lines removed. If placed in sequence in front of a mirror, the lines that were cut from the first version would reveal an apocalyptic message in Hebrew, once the vowels were removed. That was the apocryphal discovery that Rotkopf sent to Johnson, signing it with a false name, knowing that Johnson would swallow it. That was what he was planning to use to discredit Johnson during his talk."

Cuervo was waiting for you to make something of this information and, confronted by your silence, he asked:

"And?"

"And nothing."

We had arrived at the end of all the paths. We still had the locked room, a cryptic dead man, three knives, no solution, and now a dispirited Borges, a visibly tired co-decipherer of universes.

"Ultimately," you said, "the only solid thing we have is that sudden wind on the night of the crime."

"Hastur," I said.

"Hastur."

Cuervo leaped to his feet and declared:

"He is clearly the guilty party. I shall order his arrest."

Then he gave me an order:

"Come on. Borges needs to rest."

"I'll be able to rest soon enough," you said. "I've nothing planned for after my death."

"Perhaps we'll strike lucky and tonight Vogelstein will

finally remember that, somehow, Rotkopf made an S out of his reflection in the mirror, meaning 'I committed suicide'."

"I'll do my best," I said.

"Write, and you will remember," you said.

"I will, Jorge."

"The written word, Vogelstein. In order to exist, everything has to become word, everything, be it complex or simple. Think of the Universe."

"Think of 'The Gold-Bug'. Think of Zangwill's locked room."

You smiled and said again:

"Write, and you will remember."

Then you suggested that I come back the following evening. We might find all the answers we needed by plucking books from the shelves at random and choosing words blindly. You would choose them blindly, and I would read them. After all, everything was a message. Not many people knew, you said, that all your stories had been born, in one way or another, out of the eleventh edition of the *Encyclopaedia Britannica* that had been in your father's library, in the imaginary library of the King of Bohemia, ever since you were a boy. I promised I would come back. We shook hands. There I was shaking Jorge Luis Borges' flesh-and-blood hand!

Before we left, you asked Cuervo:

"What reason did they give the Japanese professor for the change of conference venue?"

"They said it was in order to pay homage to you, Borges."

"Perhaps the real target of this whole complicated conspiracy mounted in the South by the Israfel Society, and which Rotkopf's murder spoiled, was me. Apart from Poe and Lovecraft, I have written more literature with apparently hidden meanings – always so tempting to unhinged interpreters – than anyone. They must have found out that, instead of stopping or simply dying like any other sensible fellow, I was starting work on a treatise on mirrors. A highly dangerous subject, eh, Vogelstein?"

"Goodbye, Jorge," I said.

I'VE BEEN BACK IN PORTO ALEGRE FOR A WEEK, BUT ONLY NOW can I say that I have truly remembered, really and truly remembered. I have finally remembered completely, as Cuervo asked me to. I wrote in order to remember and, as you see, or as others will have seen for you, I have made a book out of what I remembered — with an epigraph and everything! A book of our meetings, Jorge, so that you can remember too.

As you know, when Cuervo left me at the hotel that evening, I met Angela, who had everything ready for my journey, even my suitcase was packed. I had no choice. We didn't have much time to catch the plane and had to run through the airport. You will be pleased to know that, as I ran, I knocked over the Japanese professor, who was also on his way home. I couldn't even stop to help him up. I left him lying on the ground, raging and railing. This will, I believe, be his last conference.

You knew who I was, didn't you, Jorge? From the moment we were introduced. You remembered my arrogant surgical intervention in your story in Mistério Magazine, the unforgivable tail, my letters, my stories. Well, I'm going to give you an opportunity for retribution. I want you to finish this book for me. Feel free to add whatever tail you care to, I won't touch a line of it. I will translate it into Portuguese, but I will change nothing, I promise. The final chapter — the ending, the conclusion, the final result of our "arduous algebra" (if I may quote you once again) in search of a solution — is all yours. This is my way of redeeming myself.

My definitive memory of the scene of the crime is as follows: Rotkopf's body in the form of a V was lying with the hands and feet against the mirror, forming a lozenge with its own reflection. The sacred triangle with one point too many facing South, the point that is missing in the Trinity. The Woman or the Devil?

The cards were as I described them the first time. The *10* (or *X*?) next to the jack, a space and then the king.

The jack's eyes had been pierced.

Now it's your turn to write, Jorge.

The Tail

My dear V.,

Thank you for this privilege, which I can only attribute to the excess of deference which only idols or the old inspire. It is very rare, in the tortuous relationship between an author and his creations, for a character to be charged with choosing the end of the story. But I suspect that the only possible conclusion is the one you determined at the outset: we never escape the author, however generous or penitent he may seem.

I did find it odd your repeated and distinctly unsubtle references throughout the narrative to "The Gold-Bug". It did not seem to me to have any bearing on the story. In the final scene, when "Vogelstein" and "Borges" say goodbye beside that improbable electric heater, you make another deliberate mistake when you cite my two examples of simple mysteries. Instead of the "The Purloined Letter" you mention "The Gold-Bug", but keep Zangwill's locked room as the other example.

I began to think about the possible relevance of Poe's story about the discovery of a gold-bug and the parchment it is wrapped in, and I remembered that, in the story, Poe, who had already invented the detective story and the parody of the detective story and the anti-detective story, was inventing one of the most controversial of all detective story conventions, that of the unreliable narrator. Although the gold-bug gives its name to the story and seems to be at the centre of the plot, it is, in fact, an unimportant detail. The parchment is what matters, for on it is the coded message that leads to the treasure. The narrator tricks the reader, who only knows what he knows at the end. By invoking "The Gold-Bug", you were telling me that the solution to the case of the German murdered in a locked room was not to be found in the clues left at the scene of the crime or even in the crime itself, but in your story. The incident was the gold-bug of your story, dear unreliable narrator, and your narrative was the parchment, wherein lies the explanation for everything.

"Vogelstein" begins his narrative by declaring his innocence, which is always suspicious. He says that he was called on by destiny to be the instrument in a conspiracy with unfathomable intentions, and that his role in the plot would be as neutral as that of the mirrors in a room. Up to that point, however, there are only two things in your story that can be believed. One is that geography is destiny. The other is that your cat died. Whether or not any conspiracy was involved, we do not know, but your personal intentions were clearly delineated from the day that your Aunt Raquel nearly fainted when she saw a photograph of Joachim Rotkopf in the pages of the Israfel Society journal or on the back flap of one of his books. It was him, the monster! The man with whom your mother had fallen in love and in whom she had trusted, electing to stay in Nazi Germany rather than flee to South America and salvation with her sisters and her small son.

I don't know if "Vogelstein" found out then that the monster was his father, or if, on that dreadful day, his Aunt Raquel told him everything. Joachim Rotkopf, or whatever he called himself at the time, had demanded that the youngest of the Vogelstein sisters get rid of her son and stay with him in Berlin, saying that he had friends in the new regime and would make sure that nothing happened to her. Miriam, the lovely Miriam of the photograph taken on the Unter den Linden on a summer's day, chose her lover in preference to her son. You were careful to include the detail of the woollen scarf worn by Miriam's lover in the photograph, in midsummer, and then to emphasise that Joachim Rotkopf felt the cold terribly and kept a fire burning in his house even during the Mexican summer. They say that one of the characteristics of demons is that they always feel cold.

It was after he learned who Joachim Rotkopf was that "Vogelstein" started corresponding with him using a pseudonym and, as a pretext, their mutual interest in Poe. He wanted to find out what Rotkopf's life had been like, what he had done during the war, how he had ended up living in Mexico under a false name and writing literary essays. Perhaps one day Rotkopf would open up to him and tell him all about his mother and how he had betrayed her. Perhaps "Vogelstein" was already thinking vaguely of revenge. But how? How could he ever get to meet Rotkopf without money, unable to travel because both his aunt and his cat needed him?

And then, one day, comes the news that the Israfel Society conference is to be held in Buenos Aires, less than a thousand kilometres from Porto Alegre, and that Joachim Rotkopf will be taking part. "Vogelstein" does not need to go to Rotkopf. The devil is coming to him! Geography is destiny.

And then "Vogelstein" discovers that the God of coincidences is on his side. His cat Aleph dies (thank you very much). While taking care of his Aunt Raquel, "Vogelstein" had learned everything there was to know about the correct use of sedatives, as you yourself noted. He still doesn't quite know how he will use this knowledge; he will know this when he gets close to Rotkopf. He buys a knife in Porto Alegre. Or perhaps in Buenos Aires. Since it is up to me to finish the story, I would like Cuervo to discover that two of the three knives, the one with the traces of blood on it and the other one found in the same ventilation shaft, Johnson's knife, were not made in Argentina. (Cuervo will continue to trust in his scientific methods even when there is no further possibility of solving the case, or, at the very least, of finding an accused.)

When he arrives in Buenos Aires, "Vogelstein" discovers that he has been assigned to the same hotel as Rotkopf, in yet another decisive intervention by the God of coincidences, this time assisted by one of the conference stewards, Angela, who — another helpful hand from fate — takes a liking to him. At the horizontal-Japanese-professor cocktail party, Rotkopf suggests to "Vogelstein" that they meet later in his room. This is the chance "Vogelstein" has been waiting for. However, they end up travelling in the same taxi back to the hotel and go straight to Rotkopf's room. "Vogelstein" does not have his knife with him; he packed it in his suitcase to avoid detection at the airport, and this is still in his room. But he does have the sedatives in his pocket, because he went to the cocktail party wearing the same jacket he wore for the journey, as you were also at pains to point out. He is not drunk, as the misleading author says in his narrative. He drank very little champagne at the party and only pretends to keep up with Rotkopf, who downs great gulps of tequila while railing against the world and its inhabitants, especially academics. It is not difficult to add a sedative to Rotkopf's tequila, just the right amount for him to be capable of locking the door after "Vogelstein" leaves the room at eleven o'clock, before collapsing on the floor, not to be woken even by Johnson banging on the door half an hour later.

I don't know when "Vogelstein" remembers "The Big Bow Mystery", Zangwill's locked room story in which the murderer is the one who breaks down the door and "discovers" the body. Perhaps it had already occurred to him before he set off, hence the sedatives and the knife. Perhaps he only thought of it once he was in Rotkopf's room, watching him drink tequila and boasting about what he intended to do the next day with the reputations of Urquiza and Johnson and the joker who writes to him. Or perhaps "Vogelstein" and Rotkopf have a father-son chat, full of revelations and guilt, and Rotkopf is forced to face up to his own villainy, so much so that he makes his moral self in the mirror try to kill him too. When "Vogelstein" tells Rotkopf to lock his door because someone might try to kill him that night, he already knows, before he leaves, what he is going to do. This locked room story will be a simple Zangwill mystery, far simpler than Poe's "Rue Morgue" mystery.

"Vogelstein" picks up the key to his room, *202*, from reception. He goes upstairs and waits for time to pass. There is no phone call from Rotkopf. Even in your unreliable narrative you made it clear that this would be impossible, given that Rotkopf could not have known the room number, since "Vogelstein" himself did not know it when he left Rotkopf's room — drunk, according to you — nor would he have been able to locate him by name, because he only knew him by his pseudonym. Your narrative is honest in that respect, my dear V.: there are several clear signs that "Vogelstein" is lying throughout.

You want "Borges" to know that "Vogelstein" is lying. When "Vogelstein" comments on my Piranesi engravings, he talks about Piranesi's ruins. But Piranesi, not content with Rome's ruins, invented other fantastical ones, and made drawings of buildings and interiors not in a ruined state, all done with great architectural rigour. And my Piranesi engravings are not of ruins, as "Vogelstein" would know "Borges" would know. When the book falls on the floor in my library, "Vogelstein" says that it has fallen open at the beginning of "The Gold-Bug". My contribution: the book is a selection of Poe's stories that does not include "The Gold-Bug". Another message from "Vogelstein" to "Borges" that he is lying.

At three o'clock in the morning, "Vogelstein" goes up to the seventh floor and starts banging on Rotkopf's door. He runs off to call the night porter, counting on more help from the God of coincidences, who does not fail him. The night porter is exactly the sort that "Vogelstein" needs: young, inexperienced and terrified. After he has helped him break down the door, "Vogelstein" does not allow him into the room, to spare him the terrible scene, and he orders him to go for help. He then creates the terrible scene that he did not want the porter to see. Rotkopf is lying on the floor, unconscious. "Vogelstein" kills him with "the slicer", then drags the body over to the mirror, leaving a sheet of blood on the floor. When other people start to come into the room, it is "Vogelstein" who directs the confusion, even suggesting that Rotkopf is still breathing and could be resuscitated, all so that no-one has the unfortunate idea that nothing should be touched. When the police arrive, "Vogelstein" has the monopoly on information. Only he can tell them about the terrible scene that greeted him when he broke down the door and before everyone else arrived. After misleading the police, the murderer goes down to his room, cleans the knife and throws it out of the bedroom window. The bathroom in room 202 also gives onto the ventilation shaft where the two knives were found.

So, in the end, there was no conspiracy or, if there was one, it became irrelevant. Johnson and Urquiza also wanted to kill Rotkopf and threw their knives away after "Vogelstein" had done the job for them. Or else Urquiza was actually ordered to kill Johnson in order to protect the secret codes that the Israfel Society does not want to be revealed, or the dead names in the Necronomicon which cannot be invoked for fear of destroying the world, or a sinister alliance forged in the library of a mad king and which crosses the centuries like the pulsating light in John Dee's speculum in the British Museum, but everything gave way to a drama even more ancient than that of Akhenaten and of Thebes and the pyramids: a son killing his father. The jack with his eyes put out fulfilling an ancient destiny.

In the last chapter of your parchment, you say that the image formed by Rotkopf's body in the mirror was a lozenge, in order to support the final speculation (a most appropriate word) that "Borges" made about the dead man's penultimate message, according to the narrator's very imprecise memory. M for mater, mother, Maria. Or, as we now know, Miriam. The South, the missing point on the sacred triangle which transforms the triangle into a lozenge, the three into four. In short, you were kind to me, ending your unreliable narrative with a gesture of filial submission, by presenting me with the lozenge and with the ability to supply the right answer. The right answer to the enigma, the right answer to everything, was Miriam. You even suggest that the right answer had occurred to "Borges" before the last scene, when I mentioned that my mother was Jewish too. "Borges" is saying to "Vogelstein" that they have

127

other things in common apart from practising the dangerous art of the written word.

If this were my story, "Borges" would, at that moment, have realised that the clues you invented were not from the murder victim, but from the murderer. And if they came from the murderer, who were they for? For him, of course. One possible conclusion is that you were merely sending me another story. Your fourth story, providing the fourth point that forms the lozenge. A story I would be unable to ignore, as I did the other three, and which would catch my attention even if only because of the sheer amount of blood. Or were you merely showing that an intellectual can use "the slicer" with all the coolness of a professional killer or of a compadre from Palermo, just to arouse my envy? Of the three knives found in the hotel, only one deserved the name of "slicer". In the hands of the other two intellectuals, the knives would have remained "blades", hypothetical "slicers", mere literature. This is "Vogelstein" saying to "Borges" that he is greater than him, greater than his idol, for he had broken through the passivity of the writer, confronted a real demon and created a real sheet of blood.

Before I finish, one more speculation. You may not have noticed that, in your story, the lovely Angela is able to leave locked rooms without unlocking the door, or was that apparently careless mistake deliberate too, just to make me speculate a little more? The Kabbala often uses angels, and she bore on her body some suspiciously symmetrical marks. Maybe "Vogelstein" really was called on to carry out a mission. They took advantage of his hatred, nourished over many years, for the man who had abandoned his mother, and so he was placed in Rotkopf's room with a knife in his hand in order to execute his personal monster and, at the same time, resolve another story or prevent another revelation. Perhaps, when he invented that mirror version of the poem "Israfel", the awful Rotkopf had chanced upon a truth, like Lovecraft discovering the Necronomicon. An accidental truth that could not be published and to which end, to prevent its being revealed, you were brought from Bonfim with your knife and your desire for vengeance. According to the epigraph to Poe's poem "Israfel" — the sweet-voiced angel from the Koran — if you remove the vowels from the name and reverse the consonants, you get LFRS, the neo-Zoroastrian Tetragrammaton. With other vowels inserted, it would become the name of a malign god that might be spoken out loud before the time was right.

And, to conclude, since I have that privilege, here's one final speculation. Do not take it as mere vanity on the part of a minor character, who, having failed as a detective, demands the glory of being a victim, but perhaps "Vogelstein's" real mission was to kill me. Perhaps the Israfel Society gathered us all together in the shadow of those powerful beings of the South, Azathoth and Yog-Sothoth, the king and the prince of chaos, in the centre of the X, so that "Vogelstein" and his "slicer" would prevent me from finishing my Final Treatise on Mirrors, which would contain the key to all my work and, therefore, to the Universe. The murder in the locked room would be a ruse to get "Vogelstein" into my library. But "Vogelstein" gave up, disarmed by my willingness to consider him an equal and to allow him to call me by my first name. All, in the end, is vanity. I was saved by my own kindness. In order to prove or disprove this version, we would have to know whether "Vogelstein" threw his knife out of the bathroom window after killing Rotkopf or after visiting me for the first time. Since the story ends here, we will never know.

129

You yourself, when you invented the four cards left on the table in the room, unwittingly provoked these final speculations. You placed the 10 before the jack simply to give the idea of a sequence and, by the interruption of that sequence, to call attention to the absence of the queen. But 10 is also X, the unknown, the Romans' double V, the hidden motive, the obscure necessity at the jack's side, guiding his hand and his knife. Just because we do not believe in these invisible beings does not mean they do not exist.

(We all have ambitions to be sorcerers. Johannes Trithemius, a famous cryptographer from the time of Maximilian I, invented an ancient historian called Hunibaldus to lend credibility to some of his theories about Germany's past. So convincing was he that Hunibaldus was included as an entry in an edition of the Encyclopaedia Britannica as if he really had existed, until the deception was uncovered and he was purged from the next edition. Johannes Trithemius is my idol. I tried, but never managed to get a single one of my false historical figures or invented authorities into an encyclopaedia, even for ten minutes.)

This is how it ends. Urquiza back in Mendoza, where he presides over sombre rituals in the subterranean church in the cellar of his castle, with the possible participation of the provincial bishop. Johnson in the United States, where he fled after refusing to answer any more questions and without being accused of anything, because there was no proof against him. "Vogelstein" in Porto Alegre, happy because he has finally got a response out of me. I and "Borges", interrupting our work on our Final Treatise on Mirrors in order to travel to Geneva, where we will die next year. Or where I will die. "Borges" will probably survive to haunt Buenos Aires for a few more years, then gradually disappear, like various other myths surrounding me. And I cannot resist the temptation, if you'll allow me, of giving the last word of this story to Cuervo. Questioned on the possibility of the case being reopened if, for example, a written confession should appear, even in the form of a novel, quoth the Raven, "Never more."

Best wishes,
Jorge

PS It is very kind of you to attribute to me, at the end of my life, sufficient energy and interest to write this letter, let alone The Final Treatise on Mirrors. By the way, the only story of mine to be published in Mistério Magazine came out in *1948*, when, unless you were a marvel of precocity, you could not possibly have translated it. Even the most fantastical of stories, my dear V., requires a minimum of verisimilitude.

JORGE LUIS BORGES WAS BORN IN BUENOS AIRES ON 24 August, 1899. When he was seven years old, he wrote his first text, in English, a language he learned from his paternal grandmother, who was born in Northumberland. He was brought up in Europe, where his family moved in 1914 and where they remained until 1921. He began his literary career in Seville, writing poetry. Back in Buenos Aires, he founded – or collaborated on – various cultural magazines, publishing poems and articles. In 1938, his father died, and Borges had an accident that nearly cost him his life, and from then on, his sight began to deteriorate, just as had happened with his father, who was blind when he died. From 1956 onwards, Borges was no longer able to read. He depended on the help of others to write, and his mother read to him and continued to do so until she died in 1975, at the age of ninety-nine. In 1939, Borges published the story "Pierre Menard, author of Quixote", his first story in the fantastic vein, a mixture of pseudo-essay and fiction, that would characterise his most famous collections of stories, for example, *A Universal History of Infamy*, *The Garden of Forking Paths*, *The Aleph*, *Brodie's Report* and *The Book of Sand*. Under the pseudonym, H. Bustos Domecq, he and his great friend Adolfo Bioy Casares published stories featuring the detective Don Isidro Parodi. As well as fiction and poetry, Borges wrote about the different districts, people and music of Buenos Aires. In 1961, he shared with Samuel Beckett a prize awarded by the International Congress of Publishers – one of many prizes and titles that he received during his lifetime. His international reputation dates from then. In 1980, he won the Cervantes Prize. In 1967, he married Elsa Astete, from whom he was divorced three years later. He was married to his collaborator, Maria Kodama, when he died in Geneva in June 1986.